BLACK S

HELL HATH NO FURY

by
David Dixon

HELL HATH NO FURY

ISBN
Paperback: 978-1-990317-07-1
eBook: 978-1-990317-06-4

Interior design by Crystal L. Kirkham
www.darkbrewpress.com

THE BLACK SUN SERIES
by David Dixon

The Damsel

Six-Gun Shuffle

Hell Hath No Fury

CHAPTER ONE

I've seen a lot of shit.

I was on Titan when the Tigers pulled off the Khalil Attack. I flew with Blackie Crisk for six months. I was a block boss in the Greens when we fought the Reds in the Skyla Sector Gang War and wound up aboard the *Braxton* in the securemax unit for my trouble. I've been in God knows how many fistfights, knifefights, and firefights—and cleaned up after God knows how many more. Between gun battles, decompression accidents, and jailhouse riots, I thought I'd seen the worst humanity had to offer.

But I was wrong.

The boss and I had just landed on Bohr Station and spent six hours arguing with what I thought at the time was the single dumbest customs officer in the galaxy—and that's a high bar.

1

"Jesus H. Christ, what was that?" the boss asked me when we emerged from the customs office. "You'd think that dude had never even seen a customs declaration. How the hell did he make general inspector?"

"Right there with you, man," I answered. "'There were discrepancies' he said. We filed an empty bay, scanned empty, and then landed at tare weight! What the fuck kind of discrepancy can there be?"

The boss shrugged. "I dunno, and to be honest, I don't care. All I wanna do is get that O2 sensor replaced and see if that offer we got to haul out to Basmallah III still stands."

"While you're doing that, I'm going to get up with Mo and see if I can score a copy of CryptoKiller that actually works this time," I told him as we boarded a public tram to docking bay Z where our ship was parked.

The boss snorted. "What are you going back to him for? He ripped us for a hundred-fifty credits the last time we were here for the copy we *do* have. That software sucks."

"Well, when you're buying pirated shit, it's hard to complain to the manufacturer, you know? And when it sells legit for like twenty-five times what you pay for it, it's hard to complain to the guy you bought a bootleg copy off of either."

The boss frowned. "I guess. But still, money is money. Get us a good deal and try not get ripped off too bad. Again."

"C'mon, man. It's me you're talking about here."

"Yeah, I know. That's why I said it."

We kept on bullshitting through our tram ride and all the way through bay Z. Right up until we realized that we'd walked literally *all the way* through the docking bay—that is, we'd walked past all sixty docking stalls and never seen our ship. The massive doors that marked the transition from docking bay Z to ZA loomed in front of us.

"What the fuck?" the boss asked.

"We were in 41Z," I said. "I remember. I swear it's 41Z."

He pulled out the receipt, which we'd never had to do before because it isn't hard to remember where you've parked the only thing you own, especially when it's a cross between your home, your job, and your crazy ex-girlfriend. Forgetting where you docked your ship is like forgetting where you left your dick—it just doesn't happen.

"It's 41Z all right."

We turned around and marched back to 41Z, where we'd parked our spaceworn Black Sun 490 between an Indus 45L and a blue Shoushen of indiscriminate model. The other two small cargo haulers were still there, but our Black Sun was

3

gone—the painted yellow square on the deck that marked our slice of real estate on the station was empty.

We walked to the center of the bay and slowly circled our way around it like absolute idiots, as if the ship could somehow be hiding in a giant open space. The boss even craned his neck to look up, just to be sure it hadn't somehow docked itself on the ceiling, although for all I knew he was looking for a camera to see if someone who had a strange desire to meet a very violent end was fucking with us.

We were so confused that we missed six uniformed Bohr security cops when they showed up from whatever hole cops crawl out of.

"Is there a problem? You two looking for something?" one of the cops asked in a voice soaked in sarcasm. I looked up and was about to let him have a smart remark but noticed that he wasn't alone like the bay guards usually were. He was rolling with a crew. My gut tightened.

The boss seemed to have no compunction about smarting off, though. Either that, or he was too stupid to realize that this was more than just general stop-and-harass cop dickishness.

"Yeah, dipshit. I am looking for something. Two things, actually."

"Which are?" the cop asked.

"Well, first, I'm looking for my ship. You know, that thing you guys are supposed to be guarding while it's parked here?"

"Haven't seen it. Sorry, can't help. But maybe we could make it up to you and help with that second thing you needed," one of the cops said with a wicked grin.

The boss nodded. "Yeah, maybe so. See, I'm looking for your mom's number. She gave it to me when I climbed off her last night, but I seem to have lost it. So if you find it, let me know, okay?"

The cop took it better than I expected, flashing an easygoing smile that his eyes betrayed as false. "Watch it. You really have no idea why I'm here."

It was my turn. "Not exactly, but let me take a few guesses: a C average? Unresolved issues from adolescence? Tiny dick? Never knew your real dad? I dunno, man, you tell us."

I had the bad feeling that this cop was going to give us a hard time no matter what, so I wanted to get in my smart-ass comments while I still had teeth.

"All right, all right," he said, still smiling. "Open mic night is over. You two can come with me the easy way or you can come with me the hard way." His squad took this as a signal to spread out in a loose circle around us.

"Whoa, whoa, whoa," the boss said, raising his hands in front of him to show he wasn't reaching for the revolver I knew was tucked into his shoulder holster. "Let's be cool about this. Since you obviously know what happened to the ship, why don't you just tell us what's going on down here and nobody has to go anywhere."

"Okay, *that's* a lot better. Finally using some sense," the cop said with a nod as he took a step closer to the boss.

I was only able to get out a garbled warning before the cop moved like a striking viper and zapped the boss right in the gut with his stun gun. He crumpled to the ground with a whimper.

The cop looked down at his handiwork, then turned to me with a wolfish grin as his goon squad took up positions behind me. I didn't see a way that my combat knife was going to get me out of this one, so I took the only prudent course a man nicknamed Snake could:

"So, I guess I'm just gonna go wherever you guys say then, all right?"

The cop's smile was real this time. "Yep," he said—right before his buddy got me with a stun gun in the lower back.

I stifled a cry but went to the deck all the same.

The cop squatted down beside me. "Your shit may play with the local yokels, but you have no clue who you're dealing with, so from here on out, you might want to keep the funny comments to a minimum." To make his point, he zapped me with the stun gun again, right in the neck. One of the goons slipped zip cuffs over my wrists and pulled them tight enough to cut off the circulation.

A windowless, autopiloted work van arrived, holographic police markings already fading to flat black, and the boss and I were unceremoniously hefted up and tossed inside. The rest of the cops, or whoever they were, climbed in after us. None of them said a word as the van accelerated, taking us God-knows-where.

———————————·

The van slowed to a stop about half an hour later. I risked a look at our captors, and they rewarded me with another taste of the stun gun. The jolt made me bite my tongue. I tasted blood.

"I fuckin' hate cops," I muttered.

That got me zapped again.

One of them threw a black hood over my head just before I heard the door slide open. Between the darkness, the blood in my mouth, and pretty much all my muscles screaming in agony after the stun gun, I wasn't exactly focused on what was around me, but I was still able to make out the boss getting the same treatment. I heard a brief struggle which I assumed was him wrestling to try to prevent them from getting his pistol. I knew better than to resist when I felt one of them draw my knife from its scabbard at my back.

They frog-marched us up a few sets of steep stairs, down hallways made of metal grating, and through what I guessed was a doorway into a quiet room. The plush carpet felt strange, and I heard a hatch close and a muffled conversation I couldn't make out. A blade sliced my cuffs off, and a hand to my chest sent me stumbling backward. In a moment of panic, I thought they'd pushed me off something high, but then I landed in a soft, supple chair.

The hood came off, and the boss and I found ourselves face to face with our antagonist.

He sat across from us, lower half and hands hidden behind a hefty desk. We gaped at him, open-mouthed, for what had to have been an uncomfortably long time.

The man had skin so pale it was almost transparent, pulled so tight as to make him look less like a man and more like a living corpse—his whole body was the kind of white usually associated with scar tissue. The veins in his head and neck spiderwebbed everywhere, and the least movement of his facial muscles was visible through his pallid skin. Adding to the general freakishness of his appearance was the complete lack of hair—not an eyebrow, not a single bit of stubble, and a dome so bald it made me wonder if he'd ever had any hair on his head at all. His eyes were a cold ice-water blue, but less like water to drink and more the kind of ice water that awaited passengers on doomed ocean liners. When they flicked from the boss to me without blinking, my skin crawled and I realized that they must be synthetic ocular implants, although they were admittedly the best I'd ever seen.

He flashed a rictus smile and opened his pale lips to reveal gleaming white teeth.

"Well, gentlemen, I trust you're over the unfortunate shock most people have when they meet me in the flesh. There is an explanation behind all of this, which you may yet get to hear—an explanation that most never get the chance to know." He spoke perfect inner-worlds Common, and his diction was as clean and accentless as a computer's. His delivery did nothing to calm my brain, which was screaming something along the lines of *run like holy fucking hell*. I risked a glance at the boss, who had a look on his face that I'm pretty sure mirrored mine: totally false bravado attempting unsuccessfully to hide our sheer, uncomprehending terror.

"But that does not matter," the pale man continued. "I did not bring you here for conversation, nor to try to move uncivilized men like you two with the pathos of my story. No, I brought you here so that I could talk to you in the most animal of languages—the language of fear."

"*Fear*?" the boss whispered.

"Yes. Fear." The man gave a smile that made me think of every serial killer in every horror holo I'd ever seen. "In ancient times, wise men used to say 'fear of the Lord is the beginning of good works.' It is much the same even now, except *now*, your good works will be inspired by a being much more tangible, intractable, and unmerciful than the deities of old—me."

My head spun. "Uh, I think you've got the wrong—"

"You do not *think*," he snapped. "You *fear*. The problem is, your fear is only surface fear, the type of unconscious unease that an animal might feel when faced with an unfamiliar predator, but this is not the fear I seek. This is not enough—not for you two."

I had no idea where this guy was going with his soliloquy, but I had a bad feeling that he was right and that I really didn't understand fear yet—and the horrifying thought that I soon would.

He continued. "No, I need a conscious fear from the both of you—not the panic of a frightened animal, but the true, deep-seated terror of the annihilation of your existence in every sense of the word."

What the ever-loving *fuck*?

He sighed. "When I considered how to *persuade* you, I tried to place myself in your situation, tried to reason out a motive to compel you to do what I ask. But I could reason nothing. So then, if not reason—fear. But fear of what?"

"I don't think this is really necessary to—" the boss said.

The man continued, unbothered by the interruption. "It could hardly be fear of danger. You two have faced and escaped death many times before, so much so that you cannot truly comprehend what it would mean not to exist. In your line of work, life is short and death quick and cheap, and so therefore life is cheap. Your lives are not valuable enough—even to you—to make you fear losing them."

I didn't like the sound of that at all. I took a quick glance around the plush stateroom, trying to see if I could make a break for it, but the goon squad had the doors covered.

The man's eyes narrowed as he continued, speaking more to himself than to us. "Perhaps pain? I could inflict pain quite literally beyond what you can imagine, but this very failure of your imagination works against me. How can a man fear what he cannot even fathom?" I wasn't sure he was giving me enough credit, really, because I could imagine some pretty painful things. "No. Pain is not the correct tool. But I know what is, because I know the very hope of your existence, which, in your cases, unfortunately manifests itself in a very tangible object."

He let whatever it was hang out there in silence for a moment.

"Your ship," he finished. "It is your ship that makes you different from everyone else, from all the landlubbing 'worms' you flight jockeys despise and look down on. It is your ship that allows you to free yourselves from the mundane responsibilities of putting down roots, that allows you to reinvent yourselves and remake your image in every little minor planet and system, from Earth to the farthest reaches of unfederated space. Without your ship, you are another planetbound dreamer without hope of escape. Just another slave unable to escape his master, another cog in a giant, uncaring machine, another speck of dust not at all dissimilar from the millions of other specks of dust on whatever worthless rock they inhabit."

The boss's mouth moved, but nothing came out.

"Plato says that a man who has never seen the light cannot appreciate the darkness. And there is the great thing about your fear — that you have seen the light. You know what it is like to live by your own rules, to leave a life behind and make it anew. You can truly *fear* the darkness, because you know the light. There is an old saying that a 'captain is god of his ship.' You two have been gods—small gods, but gods nonetheless—but I can make you mortal."

I started to feel a little defensive, seeing as how I was a hell of a lot more afraid of being killed than losing our piece-of-shit Black Sun 490, and this asshole seemed to be telling me that somehow made me unsophisticated. That said, the look of horror on the boss's face told me that while the pale man may have gotten me wrong, he'd gotten him right.

I figured I'd try to see if the creepy motherfucker across from us actually wanted anything from us, or he just got his rocks off scaring the shit out of people before he turned their skins into coats or whatever. "Okay, okay," I said as bravely as I could. "You want us afraid that you're gonna fuck us up in ways we can't even imagine—check. So what exactly do you want from us?"

He picked up a tablet off his desk and turned it to us. Onscreen were our UNF master files— crosslinked to every legitimate computer network in UNF space and accessed as the files of record by even non-federated computer systems. I knew that the master files existed, but as far as I had ever heard, there was no actual way to access the master file, only to make data calls to certain sections. Whatever database he was accessing was obviously way deeper shit than the boss and I were usually into. Below our two files was a copy of the ship's title, each one marked *pending permanent removal*.

"Removal of your records from the UNF database will remove you from every aspect of society. No trace of you will remain. Your ship, which is already impounded, will go up for auction. Of course, you will be unable to bid on it because you could not access your money nor could you have it titled to you, since you do not exist. You will have no licenses, no qualifications—not even an ID number. Even in the underworld, you will have reason to fear—how can authorities investigate the disappearance of someone who never existed to begin with?"

Our tormentor sighed and leaned back ever so slightly in his chair. "But I offer the opportunity to spare yourselves this fate."

There was a moment of silence.

I *still* wasn't sure what it was he wanted from us. I shivered at the thought that perhaps he'd mistaken us for someone else, then reality kicked in and I realized that someone this meticulous—even if unhinged—probably didn't make a whole lot of mistakes. I was still trying to work out whether that should be encouraging or terrifying when the boss piped up with a bit of his trademark defiance, as futile as it usually was.

"Bullshit. Nobody can just delete somebody out of the UNF database. I don't care what kind of hacker you think you are, it can't be done—the protocols are bulletproof. People have been trying to hack in forever. It can't be done."

This wasn't the best time for me to point out the critical flaw in his logic, but I didn't have to. The pale man did it for me, a ghoulish smile playing across his pale lips. "You're right. The system is impregnable, as everyone knows. This is the fundamental truism that underlies all modern commerce. Of course, I cannot hack *in*. Fortunately, this is unnecessary in my case, because *I am already inside*."

"But nobody has access to the—" the boss began.

"As Section Six, I have all the access I require to do what I have already done. Surely even you understand that there is no reason to break into a vault when one stands inside it already?"

My head swam. Section Six? I had trouble breathing.

Section Six?

Section Six didn't even exist! It was a catchall, made-up section of the UNF security apparatus. At most, it was a cover story for the activities of the Security Council's black-ops service, Section Five. Everybody—I mean everybody not wearing a tinfoil hat and carrying on about aliens—knew there was no Section Six. The document that gave the security directorates their names was only five sections long. Everybody knew that.

But there had always been whispers.

The Monks of Gethil were supposedly a Section Six operation gone wrong—or, depending on who you talked to, gone right. Crazies I'd met in my younger years blamed the Xiamin terraforming disaster on Section Six. I knew an otherwise sensible guy who swore up and down that Section Six destabilized the palladium market and caused the dissolution of the Indira Republic just before they joined the UNF—even after the scandal of how it happened became public knowledge and brought down the Pasco Secretariat. Section Six—if you believed the loony all-caps posters lurking on the bottoms of message boards who took great lengths to hide their identities—was an unstoppable, all-seeing, all-knowing force so powerful not even the Secretary General could stop them, if he was even cleared to know they existed. They were the fucking invisible boogeyman of UNF space and were no more real than Santa Claus, or the Easter Bunny, or the Galileo Nebula Being.

And yet.

And yet I was sitting across a desk from someone who looked like he'd stepped out of a nightmare and had access to apparently infinite resources he was going to use to fuck us up more thoroughly than killing us ever could, and who was demanding our cooperation in something before he'd even told us what that something was.

I began to reconsider my position on the Galileo Nebula Being.

I swallowed hard and decided to play dumb, which, given the circumstances, wasn't even really playing on my part. "Section Six?" I asked, trying to sound skeptical. "Section Six, huh? I, uh, didn't think they existed."

"And yet, here I sit," he said. "Although you are, strictly speaking, correct. *They* do not exist. *I* am Section Six. There were two of us in the beginning, but the other is..." He shrugged. "...no longer with us. He passed away in the same unfortunate shuttle accident that killed Secretary General Sakasvilli. Tragic, really. Anyway, with his untimely demise, there is no one else with oversight of the Section, so it is up to me to use the broad scope of my powers as I see fit and in a manner that will best benefit the UNF in the long run."

I realized then that with the full weight of the UNF and with no one to prove he existed, nobody could stop him.

He gave me a wicked grin. "So you understand, then. There is no escape from my power. You two are unmade, gentlemen, and while I offer damnation with my left hand, I offer salvation with my right."

"We get it." The boss sighed. "We fuckin' get it. So what the hell do you need us for if you've got everything already?"

"Before my partner shuffled off this mortal coil, he restricted certain... things... from me. Earlier, I explained the uniqueness of my position. There are none like me—just as there were, unfortunately, none like my now-deceased colleague. He restricted access to UNF files that I desperately desire." The anger that passed over the man's eerie features was like a violent storm raging across a barren planet, sending shivers down my spine. "There are certain people I wish to bring under my power, persons I very much wish to speak to, and questions I very much wish to have answered. You will bring me one of those people. Or suffer mightily for failing to do so."

"Who?" the boss and I asked almost simultaneously.

"You know her as Carla."

Oh fuck.

CHAPTER TWO

I risked a glance at the boss; his eyes flicked to me but then looked away. He didn't speak, so I guessed that meant he was leaving this one to me.

"Carla?" I said, as if I couldn't place the name. "Trying to recall if I—"

"I know you know her—and well," the pale man interrupted. "Do not attempt to deceive me. You lack the skills for it."

Of course I knew Carla. She was my girlfriend, in a manner of speaking. Friends with benefits, maybe. But exclusive friends with benefits—at least in my case—although perhaps due less to any moral obligation than to my strange inability to score with anybody else since I'd met her. It had been almost six months since I'd seen her last. The last time we'd actually spent any time together was after I'd passed her a message during a jump drive refit telling her that if she was anywhere within a week of Pinying, we knew a guy who was looking for a heavy to do some escort missions. Carla had shown up two days later, did the run, spent the next week in the sack with me, then the boss and I went our way and she went hers.

"Still thinking? Perhaps this will aid your memory," our captor said, touching a different tab on the tablet's screen.

The video was shot on a phone and began when someone switched it on as they placed it on the ship's cockpit instrument panel so it had a view of the pilot's seat. The hand holding the camera withdrew from the frame, then returned to make sure the camera stayed balanced. The hand disappeared again, just before I came into frame, plopping into the pilot's seat, a big shit-eating grin on my face. I knew exactly where this video had come from, and I knew what was coming, but for some reason, I sat there mute and watched, trying to think of a way out of the whole mess.

I could feel the heat from the boss's eyes as they bored into me—the ship's cockpit was our Black Sun 490's, and the seat was his.

Carla appeared onscreen next, from the left side of the seat, wearing her nearly skintight green flight suit and a tight orange T-shirt underneath that clashed with her chopped raven-black hair. She gave the camera a seductive smile. Then she straddled me in the seat, shrugged off the top of the flight suit, and pulled her shirt over her head, revealing the smooth olive skin of her bare back to the camera. I knew what came next.

"All right, all right, so I know her!" I shouted.

The pale man ended the video with a wave of his hand over the tablet.

"I knew that you knew her before I saw this, but it was kind of you to record it and leave it for my men to find when we picked your ship clean."

"Fine," the boss muttered. "So you know all about us. But listen, until you told us, we didn't even know she was on Bohr Station in the first place. So why the hell do you need us to find her for you if you already know she's here?"

The pale man arched his hairless brow. "*Why* is not your concern. Your concern is for the safety of your ship and your continued ability to fly it. You will find Carla and bring her to me. She will be in good health. I will give you both a sec card that will open every door on this station, so you have no excuses. You have ten standard days—starting today—during which not a single living thing will leave this station. At the end of that time, if she is not in my possession, my commands will automatically hit the UNF system and I will make real the fear which I have so painstakingly laid out for you."

The thought I should have had was *how the hell is he going to lock down Bohr Station for ten days?* But that wasn't the thought I had, because I had a new and totally unexpected revelation: I wasn't going to give Carla to this guy, no matter what he did to me.

That may seem like a no-brainer, but folks in my line of work are not typically known for their charity, loyalty, or good works. In fact, privateers have a reputation for being greedy, grasping, cutthroat sons of bitches who'd space their own grandmothers for a quick buck or a clean scan.

Prior to the point he'd demanded Carla, I wouldn't have disagreed. Hell, I never met my grandmother, so spacing her probably wouldn't be *that* bad. In fact, you could say that the only person I'd really ever extended loyalty to besides myself was the boss—and even he was still in circle-of-trust probationary status. But, for some reason, I found an unexpected desire that I never knew was there to protect Carla from this creepy, serial-killer-looking motherfucker.

Of course, I knew better than to tell *him* that because I knew if he got the idea I was useless to him, I'd either be on my way for a quick trip out the nearest airlock or a secret UNF black-site prison, depending on his mood. I decided to keep my newfound sense of chivalry to myself. The boss must have felt the same way, because he just gave me a look that was a cross between *what-the-fuck-have-you-gotten-us-into* and—okay, well, really that was pretty much it.

"Yeah. Sure. We'll look for her," he said with a sigh.

———————————————-

After another blindfolded—but mercifully stun-gun-free—trip out of the pale man's office and ride in the abducto-van, the boss and I were deposited in inner ring terminal section B, near Halstead's. We'd been given back our weapons, a duffel bag of clothes each from the ship, and a glossy black sec card unlike any other I'd ever seen.

The henchman who'd earlier played the lead cop was now outfitted like a shuttle pilot, with his trademark deep navy-blue flight suit and union local number. As he handed us the sec cards, he leaned close. "I want these back, so if you screw around and lose them, go ahead and save me the trouble and put a bullet in your brainpan—got it?"

"How the hell will we even get back to you when we find her?" the boss snarled.

The goon chuckled as he pulled the van door closed. "We'll know. Don't worry about that. We always know."

The van pulled back out into the inner ring traffic lane and smoothly accelerated, counter spin, then disappeared into the traffic.

The boss looked at me, face blank and unreadable. I expected him to start swearing and go off the deep end like he was prone to doing at times like this, or get all mopey and doom and gloom, but I got neither. Instead, he just scowled. I could tell it wasn't at the pale man—it was at me.

"What's that for?" I asked.

"In my seat?" he bellowed. "In *my* seat?"

I sighed. "Come on, man—does it really matter at this point?"

He ignored my protest. "I sit there like eighteen hours a day—it's my seat. It's where I live, goddamn it. I'm the pilot, it's my fucking chair!"

I couldn't resist. "Actually, bossman, it may be your seat, but it's my *fucking* chair."

"Jokes?" he roared. I sensed this wasn't our usual banter—he was genuinely enraged. "You got fuckin' jokes? We're drowning-deep in some crazy shit we don't even know anything about and you got *jokes*? We are ten fucking days from losing everything, funny guy! Your crazy girlfriend got us into this mess, and you're gonna crack jokes about you and her disrespecting me and my ship and—"

"Whoa there, ace," I snapped. "What's this 'disrespecting me and my ship' stuff, huh? I never knew you were such a big badass. Get the fuck over yourself, all right? So yeah, we did it. And next girl you get with, I'll loan out the turret—I don't give a rat's ass. Hell, if you'd fucked Kell in the turret, I wouldn't have cared." The boss glowered, and his right hand balled into a fist. "But last time I checked, we were in this shit together." I stabbed a finger in his chest. "So don't act like you suddenly grew another set of balls, because come at me like that again and I'll cut 'em off and feed 'em to you."

I slid the duffel bag off my shoulder and stared him down, waiting for him to say something. He gritted his teeth and folded his arms across his chest, almost daring me to swing. We stood glaring at each other like that for a good thirty seconds.

"Fuck this," he finally muttered. "I need a drink."

The tension at least temporarily defused, the boss and I grabbed our duffel bags and trudged into Halstead's where we grabbed a spot at the bar.

I ordered the only bourbon I could afford, and the boss got some cheap scotch. I nursed my drink and figured I'd wait for him to cool off before I said anything. He finished his drink before he finally spoke.

"So, how are we going to find her?"

I blinked in surprise.

I'd just figured that the boss felt the same way I did, that he too had no intention of giving up Carla to some crazy freak who looked like he stepped out of a nightmare. While I knew the threats had gotten through to the boss more than they had to me, I didn't think they'd gotten through *that* well.

"Say fucking *what*?"

"You heard me," the boss said calmly.

"Yeah, I heard you. I heard you just fine. I was giving you an opportunity to say something else."

"Well, I'm not."

"Because the question you should be asking is a different one," I continued. "It *should* be something along the lines of 'how are we going to get the ship back?'"

The boss scowled. "That's exactly what I said, when I asked how we were going to find her."

"Are you fucking kid—"

"Just face it, Snake. We aren't getting the ship back, and we aren't getting off Bohr anyway except through an airlock if we don't give this guy what he wants. I'm not real thrilled with going along with this dude either, and I know you like Carla, but it's either give her to him or..."

I took another sip of bourbon and set my glass on the bar. "Or what?"

"Or *what*?" the boss asked, slamming his hand down on the bar. "Goddamn it, Snake, or *that's fucking it*—that's what. It's or 'we get murdered' or 'we spend the rest of our miserable lives as unregistered rat runners until the union finds out and forgets to refill the ox tanks one run' or 'we lose everything and die of literal fucking *starvation* right here on Bohr.' That's *what*, Snake. Take your pick— it doesn't matter. If we don't give Carla to whoever that guy is, he and his Section Six guys have us dead to rights, and we lose the ship and it's over, that's what."

I shrugged. "So?"

My partner practically exploded: "So that's all we've got!"

I shook my head. "That's all *you've* got, you mean."

His face went blood red. "I don't think you understand what it took for me to get that ship," he said, almost choking on his rage.

"You never told me."

"You never asked," he snarled.

I shrugged again, as nonchalantly as I could. "Should I have? I didn't ask because I don't care."

That wasn't strictly true. In fact, I'd always been more than a bit curious as to how my always-broke friend had been able to afford any ship at all, even one as ludicrously ill-equipped as a Black Sun 490, but he'd never seemed any more eager to discuss his past than I was to discuss mine.

And now wasn't the time.

"Because I don't care about the past at all," I continued. "God knows mine's bad enough to not want to go back there. What matters is—"

"Is what? The future? 'Cause without a ship there isn't one."

"No, it isn't about the future—you think I'm naive enough to believe in a future with the way you fly?" I asked. "Hell no, it isn't about the *future*. It's about the *present*. And *presently*, Carla's the best thing I've got going, so I'm not going to help Section Six or anybody else find her if she doesn't want to be found."

"So Carla's the best thing you've got going for you, huh?" Contempt dripped from his every word. "So that's how it is, then? I give you a shot on Dunatis, make you part owner of my ship, and even fly your sorry ass around to rendezvous with your fuck buddy Carla, but when the going gets tough, it's just 'sorry, man, but you'll just have to accept losing everything you've got in life because I've suddenly developed a moral code, at least when it comes to girls I'm screwing.'"

"Fuck buddy? Carla isn't—she's—she's my—" I was suddenly at a loss for words.

The boss smiled sarcastically. "Your what? Your *girlfriend* you see maybe three or four times a year? You don't even know her last name, dipshit! What do you think she does while you're somewhere else—live in a convent? You remember that guy who looked like an underwear model who was flying on her wing when we met her on Coltrane? You think she wasn't fucking him? You think you're *that* fucking good that she never—"

"Shut the fuck up," I said, anger rising. "Just *shut up*. You don't know what—"

"You've only got one friend in this world, brother, and it ain't Carla. So if she's worth that to you, so fuckin' be it, but don't come crying to me when your heart's broke 'cause you walked in on her spread out and fucking some big-shot bounty hunter—"

It was at this point that I absolutely lost my shit. I'm usually not one to do things without thinking, but he really knew how to get under my skin, and even though I knew he was doing it intentionally, he still did it. My left hand came up on its own accord, and I slugged him in the right temple.

The blow knocked him right off the barstool.

Before I knew it, I followed him to the floor and drove one knee into his chest, my left hand around his throat—out of habit—my right drawing my knife from its sheath in the small of my back.

Funny thing is, I didn't even really care if Carla slept with somebody else—it was just the way he'd put it to me, like I was some sort of sap too stupid to see the truth. Unfortunately, my anger had overpowered my good sense, and I forgot that with one of my hands on his throat and the other reaching for my knife, he had *his* hands free.

I realized my mistake right about the time my knife made it down to his throat—when I felt the cold muzzle of his revolver under my chin. I calmly let go of his neck, but I still didn't move my knife from his jugular. I heard the metallic *snick-click* of the hammer going back and the cylinder rotating.

"Snake," he wheezed, unmistakable menace in his voice, "I'm not gonna blow your brains out all over the ceiling just on account of all we've been through, but I swear on the entire goddamned cosmos that if I ever see you again, I won't think twice. Now, get the fuck off me and get the fuck out of here."

I stood up right into the muzzle of the bartender's shotgun leveled across the bar. Bohr Station can be a rough place, even on the best of days. The bartender gestured toward the door. "You heard him," he said. "Get the fuck out."

I looked around at the rest of the patrons as I slipped my E-14 combat knife back into its sheath. There were more than a few hands resting on weapons, and I could see the almost imperceptible haze of a couple activated personal shielding systems through the cigarette smoke. I showed both my hands to the crowd and slowly reached down to pick up my duffel bag.

I slung it over my shoulder, finished my drink in a single gulp, and smiled wryly at the bartender. "I was just leaving."

CHAPTER THREE

There's a gap in what I remember after that, except going to another bar—or three—and seeing something about a "terrorist attack" that killed fifteen and the subsequent station-wide lockdown while security forces hunted for the "terrorists." Even in my drunken state, I recognized it as Section Six's handiwork. The realization that he could indeed do whatever he wanted only made me drink more.

Everything disappeared into a haze of cheap whiskey, cigarette smoke, and projectile vomiting.

When I finally came to, it was between a pair of trash dumpsters in a maintenance passage dividing two massive sections of low-rent transient housing on the outer ring of M deck. Like I heard in an old song once, it's not that anybody wants to sleep out in the gutter, but sometimes it's just the most comfortable place. And, as usually happens when I sleep in gutters, I was awakened by something unpleasant.

In this case, it was a homeless resident of the station who smelled like Satan's asshole, had more fingers than teeth, and had the distinct look of a jonesing zedhead in his eyes. Figuring I looked like an easy mark, he'd decided to try and steal my duffel bag out from under my head. Whether it was my head moving or his stench that woke me I'm not sure.

Either way, I went from passed out to fully awake in about half a second. In my haste to get it away from him, I gave him a swift kick right in the balls as he leaned above me, gently tugging on my worn green duffel bag. This turned out to be a mistake, since while my boot crushing his nuts did have the effect of getting him to let go of my bag, it also had the effect of dropping him right down on top of me, smell, bad breath, filth and all.

We struggled briefly, but he was jonesing bad and I was just hungover as hell, so it didn't take long for me to gain the upper hand. I smashed his head into one of the nearby dumpsters and left him where he lay, rasping blood bubbles through his broken nose and dreaming of little red and white autoinjectors.

I struggled to my feet, slung my filthy duffel bag over my shoulder, cursed the station's glaring artificial light, and nursed my throbbing head. I stumbled down the street and into an automated kiosk by a building entrance in search of some Hangover X or Next Day DDC.

After a brief discussion with the vending machine AI, I overpaid for Hangover X and it delivered my two tablets shrink-wrapped among six pages of warning labels that cautioned against side effects including but not limited to death, loss of feeling in limbs, numbness, sleep disorders, diabetes, heart failure, kidney failure, lung failure, brain lesions, acne, suicidal thoughts, psoriasis, pancreatic failure, testicular cancer, glaucoma, headache, dehydration, drowsiness, inability to sleep, bone mass loss, loss of appetite, weight gain, weight loss, erectile dysfunction, bleeding through the nose and eyes, gum loss, and tooth decay.

I downed them without hesitation.

While I waited for the medicine to do its work, I took stock of last night's activities and tried to remember what I could. It wasn't much. I checked my watch.

Shit.

It turned out it wasn't just the previous night I couldn't remember—*two whole days* had passed in the blissful embrace of booze. This meant, my still-throbbing head informed me, that while I'd been tying one on, the boss was probably out there getting leads on Carla's whereabouts. Not only that, some dark, unfamiliar, and particularly nasty voice—probably my conscience—reminded me, it was even possible that he'd already found her and handed her over to who I'd suddenly decided to call The Pale Man, capital letters and all—*TPM* for short.

I scowled as I smoked a cigarette and let it all roll around in my head. I needed another drink, but I wisely refrained and decided to mull over the options sober. As I saw it, I had two choices. First, I could just try to stay away from Carla in case TPM's crew was watching me and hoping I'd lead him to her. While this approach guaranteed I wouldn't inadvertently lead TPM to Carla, it also ran the risk of having my former boss find Carla before I could give her a warning, which meant she'd be in the clutches of TPM.

The other choice was to find and warn Carla before the boss did while also avoiding any kind of surveillance they might have on me. The problem with that approach was a) I was behind the boss's efforts to find Carla already because of my two-day bender and b) TPM's Section Six goons were going to be far better at finding and following me than I was going to be at losing them.

In the end, it came down to weighing the boss's natural incompetence against my uncanny inability to avoid people who had it out for me. Either way, I was gambling with Carla's life, but the question was whether I was willing to bet Carla's life on the boss's ineptitude or my own bad luck. After another cigarette, I decided that knowing my luck, this would probably be the one time everything worked out for the boss if I didn't do anything to stop it, so I would have to find and warn Carla myself.

Having given my two tablets of Hangover X time to work, my headache receded, and I followed the signs to the closest public access terminal. Once there, I waited for the guy ahead of me in the booth to finish futilely trying to download porn on a restricted terminal, then stepped in. I pulled up the Bohr Station public docking records, manifests, and arrival/departure schedules. A few minutes of searching confirmed what I already suspected: there was no record of Carla's Razor on the station.

I'd already known it wouldn't be that easy, though, because if it were, TPM would have skipped hauling us in and just picked her up himself. I racked my brain to remember any of the other ship types or names I'd seen Carla fly with before, but none of those names showed up on Bohr either. I combed through the list of ship names, hoping to find somebody—anybody—I recognized.

This time, I didn't come up empty.

A Kalsu Clipper's manifest listed a performance art installation by the name of *Manti's Girl*. I'm not one to hang out at art shows, but *Manti's Girl* I recognized. It was Jade's project. Jade and Carla had parted company for good about a year ago, so Jade's presence on the station could have been coincidence, but since TPM seemed positive that Carla was on Bohr, Jade seemed a better lead than anything else I had to go on.

Ignoring the growing line outside the booth, I checked the station net for advertisements for *Manti's Girl* and wrote down the address of the club on C deck outer ring that hosted the show. I was standing to leave when a sudden rush of horror seized me.

What if somehow Section Six was tapping into my browsing session? If they had a way to hack our supposedly unhackable UNF ID's, accessing a public terminal log would be no problem at all. If they were watching in real time, I'd just given them all the leads they'd need. I broke out in a cold sweat. I cleared my search, then went back to the manifests and picked out somebody else I knew—a guy who'd once sold the boss and I some defective slip ring seals for the turret that cost us a run and six days of maintenance to replace. I lingered long on his address page, tried unsuccessfully to look up his personal phone number, and generally hoped to key in on him as much as I could. To really sell it, I called and left a message on his business voicemail in which I explained breathlessly that I couldn't talk long, but I needed to see him desperately and that I needed to find "her."

I hoped he would get an unpleasant visit from TPM's goon squad and get the beatdown the boss and I still owed him—or at the very least, he'd sell TPM some faulty slip-ring seals.

———————————

From there, I jumped a turnstile, dodged a fare-cop, and made my way onto one of Bohr's public maglevs, taking the ride up to C Deck. The entire time, I tried to walk the fine line between using what few anti-surveillance techniques I knew and feeling utter, abject paranoia. I didn't succeed. Every time I turned around, I felt eyes boring into me. I tensed up every time anyone brushed up against me, fearing a subtly deposited RF tag or maybe even a UV skin tracer injection. Being on a station always meant everything was being watched, but usually nobody worried much because there was just too much information for Sec to use. Problem was, I wasn't dealing with usual station security. I was dealing with Section Six, and who knew what kind of tricks they had?

By the time the maglev deposited me on C deck, I was a nervous wreck and jonesing for a cigarette something fierce. I ducked off into a maintenance area to burn one. I drew the calming smoke into my lungs while I tried to figure out if I was right to worry about being followed or whether I was well and truly crazy.

As I flicked the butt away, I remembered a fellow smoker—Mo, my contact on Bohr for pirated software. He'd have as good as info as anybody on the best way around Bohr's surveillance system, and maybe even an idea of how to hack into the station's network so I could get a lead on Carla before the boss. I mentally added Mo's shop to my list of places to go after I talked to Jade.

I poked my head out of the maintenance alley and glanced down the street both ways until the gentle curve of the station walls formed an artificial horizon. A maglev blew by, but otherwise, what I could see of C deck was deserted. I darted across the maglev tracks toward a rundown, graffiti-covered building whose red neon sign identified it as the club I was looking for—The Persephone Club. I leaned up against the door, expecting it to be locked this early in the morning, but it yielded to the pressure and I stepped inside.

The club interior was nicer than I'd expected, given its exterior. The floor was glossy and reflective like a black mirror, coated in what I recognized as that annoying kind of polymer you can run a current through and have it change colors with the music fast enough to give somebody a seizure. The bar lay off to my left, an impressive-looking structure in polished steel, black marble, and blood-red lighting. The house lights and annoying background trance music were low, but shining out of the murk were a pair of powerful spotlights, one blue and one searing white, which I recognized from the one time Carla and I had attended Jade's show, back on Coltrane.

"Hey, Jade, you over there? It's Snake, Carla's, uh, friend," I called into the blinding spotlights.

"What?" Jade called back, a little louder than necessary.

I took a couple of steps forward into the darkness toward the glare of the show lights, hand over my eyes to shield against the brightness.

A shadow fell across me as Jade's silhouette materialized out of the light. She whispered something to a watch on her wrist, and the spotlights dimmed enough for me to make her out.

She frowned, and her eyes narrowed as she pulled a pair of earbuds from her ears. She gave a long sigh and raised an expectant eyebrow. "Oh, it's *you*? Fucking great."

"Jesus, Jade, give me a break. This isn't a social call."

"No shit," she muttered.

I took a step toward her and felt fabric under my feet.

"Careful!" Jade snapped. "I just put down three coats of metallic green on this backdrop, and if you take one more step and mess it up, I'll have Yontel throw you out on your ass."

"Look, I need your help," I said as I took a step back off whatever I'd stepped on. "This is serious. I need to talk to—"

"I don't know what else to tell you, Snake," she interrupted. "I already told your boss everything I knew."

Shit.

"Oh, and next time don't send him," she continued. "I know I've got a nice pair of tits and all, but I hate having him stare at me like he's never seen boobs."

Not only had the boss already been here, but it looked like he'd made his usual good impression.

"Uh, Jade, listen. There's a bit of a problem, see? I need to talk somewhere, ah, where nobody can hear. There's some serious shit going down, and Carla's in the middle of it."

"What? That's not what he told—"

I held up a hand. "Yeah, I know, but I'll explain."

"Fine." She sighed. "Follow me, but don't step in that paint, or there'll be hell to pay."

I followed her through a doorway that led to the club's kitchen, taking care to avoid the bright green paint.

I coughed a little uncomfortably as the kitchen light revealed that Jade was wearing what was probably considered high fashion in whatever artsy circles she ran in, but I couldn't help noticing that it exposed her left breast, and she was right—she did have a nice pair. No wonder the boss got distracted.

Her eyes narrowed. "Don't you start too—you know, I kinda only half mind him, but you I *hate*, so don't push it, all right?"

I shrugged like I had no clue what she meant. "What?"

"Don't fucking '*what*' me, Snake. What's going on?"

"Somebody big, and I mean so-big-you-wouldn't-even-believe-me-if-I-could-explain-it big, is looking for Carla. I don't know why, but he is. He's got pull like you wouldn't believe and a sadistic streak a jump wide. Trust me when I say you absolutely do not want to know anything else about him, for your own safety." The color drained from her face. "Anyway, he's got us by the balls.

We got ten—no, eight—days left of stationwide lockdown to deliver Carla to him, else he deletes our UNF ID's, scraps the ship, and pretty much fucks us in ways that haven't even been invented yet."

Jade closed her eyes and shook her head. I resisted the urge to look down at the rest of her again.

"I always knew she was running, even when she said she wasn't," she whispered, more to herself than me. Her eyes opened, ablaze with fury. "She'd always said she had something in her past she never wanted to think about again, but she never told me what it was."

"Well, if this is what she's running from, I can see why," I said, remembering TPM's threats of unimaginable pain. "So now you know. Anyway, so my boss—former boss—and I had a disagreement, right? I say fuck it, we're not giving Carla up, and he says we've got to find her. And so now he's out looking for her to turn her over to our heavy, and I'm trying to find her to warn her to get the hell out of here."

"So, he wants to turn her in and you don't want to, and that's why he was in here not a day ago telling me not to talk to you if you come in?" Her tone was sharp and bitter, a verbal poison-tipped stiletto sliding between my ribs.

"Uh, yeah, pretty much."

"That's it?"

"Yeah." I winced.

She raised a skeptical eyebrow and didn't speak.

Man, *fuck* feminine intuition.

"I mean, yeah, that is *pretty* much it. Well, that and I, uh, basically sucker-punched him at the bar after an argument about it, and I've been kinda drunk for the past two days," I admitted.

The glare she gave me could have withered a rain forest.

"Fucking men, I swear. Even when they're on a quest to save the proverbial damsel in distress, they can't help but have a dick-measuring contest in a public place, then get stupid drunk, and then eye-fuck the best friend of the very damsel they're trying to save."

I shrugged. "At least I'm trying right?"

She shook her head. "No. You see, you pathetic piece of shit, none of your misguided and certainly unfamiliar good intentions will do Carla any good if you're a worthless, stupid, incompetent bastard. And you are definitely that." Her lips pressed into a thin line, and she stared daggers at me for a second or two. "And you're serious, right? This crazy heavy really is looking for Carla?"

I nodded. "Yeah. And I'm really the only thing that stands between her and this guy, so any help you could give would be much appreciated. Especially if you've already told the boss."

She swatted me right across the face with more force than I would have expected. I started to say something when her other hand clubbed me in the left ear. I put up my arm to stop her, but she continued wailing on me as she yelled at me.

"You stupid, fucking *dick*!" she shouted. "If you wouldn't have gotten drunk out of your mind, then *you'd* be ahead of him instead of the other way around! I've already told him what I know! I didn't know she was here, but she told me she was doing some contract work for the Rise in sector the last time I talked to her, and that was only like a week ago! She told me she was working for some crew out of Parins Post, but that's all I know!"

With that, she put her head in her hands, and I thought that perhaps the tirade was over. But, as is occasionally the case with my judgments on female behavior, I couldn't have been more wrong.

"Get out! Get the fuck out!" she screamed as her head snapped up. She swung at me again, besting my attempt to dodge and landing another punch, this time just under my right eye. "If something happens to Carla, it'll be your fault, Snake! And if it does, I swear to fucking God, I will get a gun and blow what few brains you have out the back of your useless head!"

She followed me to the front door, alternating between crying hysterically and bellowing threats at me that let me know—just in case I'd forgotten it—that I'd fucked everything up royally.

I emerged from the club, blinking in the station's regular lights.

That was two people in the last three days who'd now pretty much kill me on sight. Awesome.

The only solace I could find was that I didn't really know that many more people to piss off.

CHAPTER FOUR

I returned to the nearby maintenance passage and smoked another cigarette, taking mental notes of the few people who walked by. A guy in a tan suit looked vaguely familiar from the train, but when he didn't so much as glance down the alley in my direction, I wrote it off as paranoia.

Meanwhile, I tried to suss out anything from Jade's information I could use. The word "Rise" only meant one thing to me: an H115 sector gang that operated quasi-legal side businesses to generate enough money for bribes to cover their completely illegal main businesses. And by "illegal main business," I mean smuggling and theft with the occasional foray into blackmail and murder. I'd never heard they had a presence on Bohr Station, but then again, the H115 was only two jumps away, so it wasn't hard to believe.

At first, I was tempted to write off that lead because it didn't seem like Carla's bag, but the more

I thought about it, the more I was forced to admit that while I "knew" Carla in the Biblical sense, I didn't really "know" her in the social sense.

Maybe the boss had a point earlier. She had her life, and I had mine. Since we were both in the privateering business, we crossed paths whenever the trade winds blew us to each other or when we had enough time or money to work in a visit—in other words, not often. That said, when we were together we fucked like rabbits.

I pulled myself back to the task at hand. If Carla *was* working for Rise, it wouldn't be an easy job figuring out where she was. Rise—like most criminal organizations—didn't have much patience for people poking around in their business.

I considered the possibility that maybe "Rise" was a ship name or part of one. I needed to get back to a terminal or net cafe, preferably the shadiest one I could find, and hope that all the hackers' brags about proxies, firewalls, torrents, and signal sat bouncing were true. Mo was the obvious first choice for anonymous net browsing, but his hours were always hit or miss, and since the boss was already ahead of me, I figured I'd test the ship name angle first. Besides, there was no rush to get to Mo. The boss had never even met him.

I took an elevator up to A section, A deck, outer ring, which was pretty much the shittiest district in

Bohr: cramped residential blocks, low-rent storefronts, and a constant, grating buzz due to its proximity to station life support and power-generating systems. I stepped off the elevator with a couple of other lowlifes, but I still couldn't shake the feeling that somebody was watching me. I tried to do the old holo trick of looking in a reflective store window to see if somebody was following me, but it wasn't long before I realized that between the graffiti and illegally posted signs, there weren't any reflective windows left up on A deck.

I ducked inside the sketchiest net cafe I saw, paid my fee in cash, and took a spot in a corner booth where I could keep an eye on the front door. Ignoring all the pop-up ads for illegal shit, I pulled up the station shipping records again.

I searched for "rise" as part of a ship name and got two on the inbound freighter list. The second one, a ship named *Rise of the Gryfe*, jumped out at me. Not only was "Gryfe" trademark Rise lingo for a planned hit on an enemy, but listed in its docking info was a gem: *"This ship docks at a privately held and maintained docking bay on Bohr. Private bay owners' information disclosure about ships docked at their bays is voluntary, and Bohr Station does not guarantee the accuracy of private bay information. Contact the bay owner for further inquiries."*

I smiled. It looked like Rise was involved, whether Carla had been referring to a ship or the gang itself. If she was escorting them, they'd probably let her use their bay, which meant her Razor wouldn't even appear on the station records—explaining how she could be here but not show up in a public info request. Unfortunately, Bohr Station's little blurb about contacting the bay owner for "further inquiries" wasn't going to work in this case, as prying into Rise's business was like slitting a wrist and then going swimming with the sharks.

I glanced around and sized up the collection of scum in the cafe. Surely somebody there knew which bay belonged to Rise and might let that information go for a couple of bucks. I took a Bohr Station ten-credit note out of my pocket and sauntered up to the counter.

I smoothed it out nicely in front of him. "I need to find out some info about somebody's private dock, but I don't exactly want to ask the owner," I told the grubby clerk.

He shrugged and his bushy eyebrows rose, but he took the money. "Hmmm. There's probably some folks you could ask around here, if you had the right introduction."

I fished another bill out of my pocket. "I'd like that introduction, if you could make it."

Fifty credits and two conversations later, I had the info I needed — docking Bay 417, bay block 6, M deck.

Even better, I traded two packs of cigarettes for a ride on a maintenance shuttle that dropped me off at block five, with the warning that block six wasn't friendly to strangers and my promise that whatever info I'd gotten, I didn't get from them.

Massive bulkheads divided the ring into separate bay blocks, each with its own maglev station and a pair of streets for truck and maintenance traffic. As soon as I stepped out into block five, I knew strolling innocently into block six like a lost tourist was out of the question.

Two guards, each the size of a mountain volcano and likely with tempers to match, leaned against the bulkhead next to the pedestrian lanes. I pretended to read a tram schedule and gave them the once-over out of the corner of my eye. Obvious bulges under their coats told me they were armed, and a faint haze around them revealed personal shielding systems. No one on foot dared get close to them, and I noticed that the station tram zipped past the block six stop without slowing down.

Fuck.

Block six was locked up tight.

It was time to test the card TPM had given me a couple of days ago and see if it really could unlock any door in the station. I pulled my duffel bag tight on my shoulders and moved on to plan B. That is to say, no real plan at all.

I wandered back down a side corridor until a quick glance down the hallway told me no one was looking. I pulled out the black sec card TPM had given me and swiped it through the card reader on a door marked *"Restricted Access, Bohr Station Security and Emergency Services Only."* The lock let out a little metallic *snick*, the door swung open, and I let myself in.

I found myself somewhere between the station's outer wall and the inner atmospheric containment wall. The air was far cooler, and the sound of rushing water in the station's sewer echoed around me alongside the constant buzz of high voltage electricity from station wiring. In the darkness ahead, illuminated by red security lights, the long catwalk I stood on ended in a steel blast door stenciled *"BLOCK 6."*

The curve of the station towered above me like a mountain before it disappeared into murky darkness, and when I looked over the catwalk, the only thing below me was a vertigo-inducing canyon of maintenance catwalks curving alongside the station wall. I frowned. The darkness and isolation of the place wasn't helping my mood at all.

I made my way to the door and pressed my ear against it, hoping to get some clue as to what might be on the other side. I couldn't hear anything over the hum of the station's electrical grid. I muttered a few curses about the boss, TPM, and the universe in general as I slipped my knife out of its sheath.

I hoped like hell that it opened into the same sort of little-used corridor it did in Block 5 and that I wasn't about to make some sort of grand entrance into a mob poker game or something. Keeping my knife in my right hand, I swiped Section Six's black keycard with my left.

The door opened without a sound, swinging freely into a pitch-black room.

While it wasn't quite what I'd hoped for, it *was* better than the poker game possibility. I slipped inside and pushed the door as far closed as I could without letting it relock.

In the still, quiet darkness, every heartbeat sounded like a bass drum in my ears, and my breath seemed loud enough to wake the dead.

It only took me a second or two to realize that while I may have been able to hear my heart pounding in my ears, that wasn't *my* breathing. *Oh, fuck.* There was somebody else in there with me, and they were trying to be just as quiet as I was.

Oh shit oh shit oh shit oh shit. I wondered if the stories of crazy Rise enforcers so far gone from drug use that they literally *ate* people were true.

As I waited there in the dark, willing my heart to stop thumping and trying to hold my breath without passing out, a sudden burst of clarity hit me—whoever else was in there with me had most likely gotten there the same way I had, which was why they were trying to hide, just like me.

Half a second later, I realized that the only other person besides me likely to be sneaking into a Rise-controlled docking bay through a restricted access corridor was most likely my former friend, partner, and boss.

That put me in a bit of a bind, really, seeing as how we'd parted under less-than-ideal circumstances, and even my forty-eight-hour drinking binge hadn't been enough to wipe the memory of the boss's final threat to kill me if he so much as saw me again. On the other hand, we were on pretty even footing, since we really couldn't see each other, and it would be hard for him to shoot me without attracting too much attention from the Rise members no doubt prowling around in the docking bay.

I wondered if maybe, *just maybe*, this was the chance to get him to see things my way.

I waited until I heard his breath slow, figuring that if he weren't amped up on adrenaline, he'd be more in the mood to listen to reason.

"Boss?"

Before I'd even gotten the word completely out of my mouth, I realized just how fucking incredibly wrong I was. For some reason, in the face of all my previous experience with him, I'd naively assumed that the boss would realize, *logically*, that making loud noises while secretly trying to infiltrate the property of an organized crime syndicate would be a bad idea. Because that would make sense, see?

But no.

I hadn't even finished saying the word when the room lit up like a lightning strike and there was the ear-splitting *boom* that was my partner's revolver firing, followed by the instant eardrum-bursting whip-crack of .45 inches of lead speeding past my right ear faster than the speed of sound.

Before he could get a second round off, I dove back through the door and hightailed it across the maintenance catwalk to block five as fast as I could move. Behind me, I heard shouted profanity, another shot followed by a scream, then heavy footfalls on the catwalk. The security door slammed shut with a thud that shook the catwalk underfoot. I ran even faster, if that was possible.

I was more than halfway across the catwalk when another round snapped past me and thudded into a mass of wiring on my left.

"Jesus fucking Christ, man! I'm already running away!" I yelled as loudly as I could without breaking stride. "Save your ammo for somebody who really needs it, goddamn it!"

The footfalls behind me slowed. I glanced over my shoulder but didn't stop running.

He'd slowed to a walk. "Snake?"

I pushed open the door to block five and risked turning around to face him as I stepped through. He stood in the middle of the catwalk, a puzzled look on his face and pistol in hand—far enough away for me to feel pretty confident his inaccurate ass couldn't stamp me with another shot.

"Who else would it be, you stupid asshat?" I taunted across the chasm. "Seriously. Who the fuck else would call you 'boss' when they met you in a dark room? Certainly wouldn't be one of your ex-girlfriends."

His face went from bewilderment to rage, and I swung the door shut just in time to hear the next round slam into it.

I ran pell-mell for the maglev and made it inside just before the doors closed.

CHAPTER FIVE

I stewed on the train—that asshole shot at me, and not just once or twice, but three times.

So that's the way things were going to be?

Not only did he shoot at me, but the ruckus his dumbass shooting caused had probably ruined my chance to try to find Carla or some trace of her in Rise's docking bay. After all that, Rise would be in super-paranoid mode, and anybody they even *suspected* of snooping into their business would be cruising for a quick trip out the most convenient airlock or a little bit of lead poisoning administered through the forehead.

As the station slid past the maglev windows, I stared out and scowled at my reflection. The boss had ruined all my detective work, and even worse, the motherfucker had done it by being one step ahead of me, which bothered me even more than the gunfire. I muttered curses under my breath and tried to ignore the small voice screaming at me again that if I hadn't gotten blackout drunk for two days, I wouldn't even have to worry about him having the upper hand.

I racked my brain as I rode the train to nowhere and went over what I knew, which wasn't much: a) the boss's threat to shoot at me whenever he saw me was apparently more than just colorful language, b) Rise was going to be pissed off something royal, and c) fact b) was really inconvenient seeing as how I needed to get back into that damn docking bay.

Oh, and d) TPM was still out there, and I was running behind both the boss *and* time in finding Carla. The sudden thought of The Pale Man gave me chills. I scanned the train car for any signs of his goons, but no one looked out of place. Everyone was absorbed in reading their tablets or watching a holo on their glasses. But that didn't make the paranoia go away.

One thing was clear, though—since I was being trailed by TPM's invisible agents of malice incarnate, running against my own best friend and the clock, and trying to pry into the business of one of the most notorious gangs in the sector, I'd need to change a few things up to tilt the scale back in my favor again.

I was going to need some firepower.

Back in what I used to refer to as the "Old Snake Days," I'd learned that if I needed to do something nasty and was close enough to use a pistol, I was usually close enough to use a knife. I'd also learned that for some reason, even people who didn't flinch at being shot at found the idea of having their guts ripped out in front of them via a cold steel edge absolutely terrifying. Ever since then, I'd carried my E-14 combat knife. Pistols, I'd decided—and never met anybody who could prove me wrong—were for poseurs who want to look tough but were too chickenshit to do their business with a knife like a real man.

To me, a rifle is really the only gun worth carrying. Problem is, there are some obvious limitations to walking everywhere with a long gun, which is why I didn't. But none of that really mattered any longer. If I was going to have any hope of warning Carla, much less surviving the whole insane mess, it was time for the gloves to come off. I needed a piece, but not some measly pistol. Nope, I needed a real turn-'em-inside-out, blood-and-guts-everywhere, "time to go meet the Lord, motherfucker" sort of rifle.

I had no clue where to get one on Bohr, but I knew who would—Mo.

Not only could Mo help me get a gun, but I knew I wouldn't run into the boss there, and I couldn't see a way for TPM to know anything about Mo either, as Mo and I had always scrupulously avoided any kind of traceable transaction in the past. While my primary business with him had always been software piracy, I was pretty sure copyright infringement was the least of Mo's crimes, and I felt reasonably sure that of all the limited places I could run at the moment, Mo's would be the safest.

It took two more trains and a long walk spent trying to scope out whether I was being followed to get there, but eventually I made it into the seedy-looking storefront reading *Mohammed's Electronics and Software* that marked the entrance to Mo's shop, an illegally modified cross-ring location that made it possible to walk into the building on B ring and exit on C ring.

The store was locked, as it always was. I pressed the buzzer and got no response, which wasn't unusual. In the past, I'd spent an hour or more waiting outside for Mo to let me in while he finished business with other clients or got his shit together or hid his drugs or whatever the fuck else always took him so long. But this time, I didn't have time to wait. I pulled out TPM's black super access card and swiped it. The door locks clicked, and I let myself in.

I made my way through his waiting area—a sea of circuit cards, darkened screens, computer parts, and what may have been the complete neural network from a GM-Mitsubishi HT560. In the next room, where we normally did business, Mo sat at a cluttered metal desk performing what was most likely an illegal transfer of AI personalities across a pair of holographic memory units.

He looked up in surprise and alarm when my shadow crossed the desk.

"Snake, how the hell did you get in here? I could swear that door was locked..."

I shrugged. "I got my ways, Mo. Don't sweat it. I need—"

"Ha ha, that's cute," Mo said without warmth. "Seriously, Snake. How the fuck did you get in here? My front door is all that's between me and Sec or, even worse, between me and some desperate and likely broke-ass customers like yourself, so when I ask you how you got past my lock, I'm not making polite conversation, okay?"

"Jesus, man. Chill the fuck out, all right?" I slouched into the only space available on a ratty couch piled high with circuit boards. "I'm in some trouble and through a long story you *really* don't want to know, I wound up with one of these." I held up the black security card TPM had given me.

I'd expected Mo to be impressed and maybe even mystified. Instead, the color drained from his face, his jaw dropped, and he leapt away from his desk so fast he dragged a pile of computer hardware off onto the floor.

He bolted out the door behind him and into a darkened hallway. While I wasn't sure what had spooked him so badly, I figured whatever it was might be key to my long-term survival.

I took off after him.

"Mo!" I yelled down the hallway to his back as he sprinted away from me. "Mo! What the fuck, Mo? C'mere and tell me—"

He ducked into a dimly lit room farther down the hall. I followed him inside and immediately tripped over a large plastic shipping crate he must have knocked into the doorway as he darted into the room—which turned out to be pretty damn fortunate, because as I stumbled, I caught a glimpse of Mo out of the corner of my right eye.

His trembling hands held what I recognized as a very-antique-but-still-quite-deadly double-barreled shotgun.

Well, shit.

Since I was already falling, there wasn't much I could do to get to the floor any faster, aside from wishing *really really* hard that I was already there.

The shotgun's deafening blast was followed by the *ping-ping-zing* of pellets smashing through metal computer components and ricocheting off the shop's metal walls. Fortunately for me, I hit the floor alive and unharmed save for what were gonna be some bad bruises on my forearms.

I resisted the urge to jump to my feet and slit his throat only because I couldn't be sure if Mo had fired both barrels or just one, and I didn't want to jump up just to get my brains blasted all over the room if he had another shot left. Instead, I stayed facedown on the floor and played dead, hoping Mo would think he'd hit me, even though I wasn't leaking blood all over the place.

Mo took a step forward, and even in the dim room, there was enough light for me to see his left foot step just inside my outstretched right arm.

"S-S-Snake?" he asked, voice quivering. "Snake? Are you…? D-d-did I just...? Oh shit… Oh fuck, man…"

Mo was no less of a crook than me, but he was apparently much less familiar with violence.

I was pissed. Getting shot at was part of the job description, but getting shot at multiple times in the same day by people I knew was just too fucking much. Mo may not have been familiar with violence yet, but I was about to arrange an introduction. He cracked open the shotgun to reload. I made my move.

I grabbed his left foot with my right hand and yanked it toward me. Simultaneously, I exploded off the floor with all the strength and speed I could muster. His leg came out from under him, and he toppled backward into a pile of cardboard boxes, metal crates, and circuit cards.

He screamed something incoherent as he landed and tried to scramble to his feet, but it was too late. In a flash, I was atop him, my knee in his chest, and my forearm to his throat. Mo gasped for breath, his wide, panicked eyes threatening to bulge out of his head.

"You almost shot me, you fucking assclown, and I've kinda had enough of that shit for today," I seethed as I put even more pressure on his airway. "I ought to feed you that shotgun, motherfucker—you got about two seconds to explain before I choke the ever-living shit outta you."

I let off just enough to let him draw in a ragged gasp of breath.

"I-I-I'm… sorry, Snake," he managed to choke out. "But that card! You gotta get rid of that card! They'll be here any minute! We gotta—gotta—get out of here!"

"What the hell are you talking about?" I let go of his throat, but I kept the knee pinning him to the floor.

"Just give it to me!" he rasped. "Give it to me, then I'll explain!"

I jumped up, yanked him off the floor by his collar, and dragged him out the door into the hallway by the throat. "Which way?" I asked. "Where to?"

"This way," he said with a jerk of his head farther down the hall in the direction we'd been running before he'd ducked into the room. I dragged him down the hallway. "Right here! Right here!" he said when we reached the next door. "Give me the card!"

I handed it to him, and he pushed open the door to a small, filthy bathroom where he promptly tossed it into the toilet and flushed it before I even grasped what was going on.

I blinked in surprise.

"What the *fuck*, Mo?" I sputtered as it disappeared. "They're gonna kill me for that!"

I took a menacing step toward him.

He took a step backward, back flat against the bathroom wall, raising his hands in front of him. "Just—just—hear me out, Snake."

"Start talking, and make it good, or else you're following that card down this toilet with the rest of the shit, got it?"

"Look, Snake, I don't know where you got that card, and I *promise* I don't want to, okay? But that card is—I mean, I've never even *heard* of somebody who's ever even claimed to have actually seen one for real, and I've forgotten more about Sec than you've ever known. That card is the baddest of bad juju, Snake. That card is a fucking nightmare—it's a fucking basilisk card for Chrissakes!"

I hate it when people explain shit in a way that makes the whole thing more complicated than it was to start with. I wanted to punch him in his stupid face, but I knew it wouldn't help anything. "And what the *fuck* is a basilisk?"

"It's a mythological creature that kills you when you look at it, that's what the fuck it is. In the hacking world, we call it a basilisk card because you're dead if you ever see anybody who's using it. Hell, before you brought that thing in here, I didn't even think they really existed!"

"Why? I mean, what's it do? And don't try to bullshit me, or else I'm gonna make that story about dying when you see one a *lot* more believable," I warned.

Mo put his head in his hands. "You don't even know what it does? Then why are you carrying it around, you dumb motherfucker? It's the highest possible level encryption breaker—it'll unlock any door with a keycard system. The rumor is some super secret, crazy-ass, hacker-cyber-ninja branch of Section Five makes 'em, and they get issued to their fuckin' ghost squads that hunt people down and ghost 'em. Get it?"

"The truth is even worse than you know," I muttered. "But why flush it?"

"Are you really that stupid, Snake? Just think about it for a second, you knuckle-dragging moron!"

"Look, asshole, it's been one of those days, and I'm kinda all thought out at the moment, so how about you just answer my fucking question."

"Fine. I'm going to try to explain this in very small words for you, just so you can understand. Everything it opens, it logs and tracks. But that's not all. That fucking thing also activates any Sec surveillance nearby—in real time. It's like a giant, unmissable finger lit up in fucking blinking neon pointing *right at you*. Everywhere you go, that thing is screaming out to them exactly where you are and what you're doing. That make sense, or do I need to draw you a picture?"

My world spun. So much for me trying to sneak around and avoid surveillance.

"And, *oh by the way*," Mo said with perhaps a little more anger than was smart given his situation, "you brought that... *thing* to me. To *my* shop, which means I'm either out of business or in jail. Or both. So thanks. A lot."

"You told me one time that you'd disabled everything in here." I gestured to the surrounding walls. "I thought you said this place was safe!"

"Yeah, sure I did, Snake, but I was talking about Bohr Station Sec, man, not whatever high-level heavy shit you got going down. There's probably access below root level with that thing—has to be, actually, since you opened my front door with it—and God only knows what it's turned on that me or Station Sec probably didn't even know existed."

I blinked. "Shit. We gotta get outta here."

"Yeah, you think?" he said bitterly. "That's what I was trying to do."

"All right, fine," I agreed. "Let's fuckin' go then. You lead the way, but not too fast, 'cause I'm coming with you, and I've still got my original reason for coming to see you in the first place."

I let him slide past me and followed him to a door at the end of the hallway. From there, we tracked through a maze of rooms and passages until we emerged into a maintenance alley on what I recognized as C deck. I still didn't breathe easy until we'd scrambled across the maglev track and into a seedy-looking bar built against the station's outer wall and I had a lit cigarette in my hand and a beer on the table in front of me.

"Before we talk about anything else, just answer me this," Mo demanded from across the dirty booth. "Do you have any other surprises up your sleeve? Anything else you need to tell me? Fucking the Secretary General's wife on the side? Running guns to the Titan Tigers? That sort of thing? Who the *fuck* did you kill to get that card?"

"Huh?" I asked. "I didn't kill anybody for that card, Mo. One of those crazy secret agent assassin types gave it to me."

Mo's bushy eyebrows rose. "They gave it to you? For what? They got somebody you're supposed to kill or what? You seem way too stupid to be the UNF contract type, unless you're really, really, *really* deep under cover—in which case, I'm totally sold."

"Shut the fuck up, Mo. The truth is... complicated." I thought for a moment before I continued. How was the best way to explain it all without sounding like a lunatic who'd escaped the asylum? "Okay, so, uh... Basically there's this guy who is—well, he's the kind of person who would have access to that card. He's got me by the balls. He wants me to find somebody for him or else...

and he gave me that card supposedly to help me find that person."

"So what the fuck are you coming to me for, you dumb fuck?" Mo hissed. "Go find whoever it is you're looking for and leave me out of it!"

"That's the problem, see? I don't actually want to help the heavy find the person. I'm trying to find and warn—"

"*Warn* them? Say fucking *what*?" Mo asked. "And then what's the plan after that?"

I shrugged. "I haven't really thought that far out."

"Why don't you just take a nap out there on the tracks?" He pointed out to the maglev rails we'd crossed. "It'd be a lot simpler and probably less painful. What the hell do you think they're going to do to you when they find out—and they will, you dense motherfucker—that you've warned their target off, huh? You think they're just gonna shrug it off, snap their fingers, and say, 'oh, goshdarnit, good ol' Snake sure pulled one over on us'? You think that's gonna be how it goes down?"

"No," I snapped. "But I don't care, I'm not giving her up to—"

"Did you just say *her*? Is that what I heard?" Mo put his head in his hands. "This is over a girl? Oh, sweet Jesus…"

"I thought you were Jewish—I didn't think you said *Jesus*," I pointed out.

His head came up. "Snake, you think I'm *Jewish*? What exactly do you think *Mo* is short for, you fucking idiot?"

I shrugged.

"Mo is short for *Mohammed*, idiot! I'm Muslim, not Jewish!"

"They're not the same thing?" My knowledge of ancient religion was a bit spotty, admittedly.

"I wish you'd gotten hit by the train on the way over here, Snake, and saved me both the trouble of losing my business and the complete waste of my time that is this conversation," Mo told me matter-of-factly. "You are absolutely the stupidest person I have ever met."

"You need to meet more people," I told him. "You'd change your mind pretty damn quick. But I really don't care what you think—I came to you for some help, and I'm gonna get it."

"Well, you are shit out of luck, Snake. I'm not going back in there and helping anybody—least of all somebody who's on the run from some kinda crazy UNF black ops squad. If you need something from the shop, go get it yourself. Go ahead and take your chances, but you just blew me and everything I've done wide open. I'm gone. I'm clearing out the emergency account, activating the clean ID, hacking in and doing a records purge, and then I'm off Bohr forever as soon as they lift the blockade. I'll probably have to leave the sector. I suggest you do the same." He gave a bitter, suspicious look. "Oh yeah, and don't ever mention me or my name to anybody you meet. Ever."

My heart leapt. "Hey! Could you make me an ID if mine got lost—"

"Of course," Mo said. "Yeah, I could make you a new ID. I mean, I *won't*, but I could. We do it all the time. New ID cards are easy to forge. All anybody needs is your UNF master file ID number, and then it's as simple as—"

"What if I didn't have a master file ID?" I interrupted.

He rolled his eyes. "That question makes no sense, Snake," he told me in a patronizing tone. "There's nobody without a master file ID—there's no way. That's just not possible, man. I mean, if you could somehow—and this is only a thought exercise because you absolutely cannot do what I'm about to describe—but if *somehow* you could hack in and delete somebody's master file, they'd be totally and irrevocably fucked. They couldn't do *anything* once you'd gotten them that good. They couldn't even make a clean ID because they'd have no master biometrics record to tie it to. Heh. Now, *that* would be a good trick…"

I didn't think it was nearly as interesting as Mo did, but it did confirm that TPM's take on the situation was pretty much dead on.

Awesome.

"Forget about that," I told Mo. "I didn't come to you looking for computer help. I came looking for a gun." He opened his mouth to protest, but I shook my head. "And, yes, I know you don't have any guns because if you did, you'd have killed me instead of just scaring the shit out of me with that goddamn antique you had back there. I just need a contact for how I can get my hands on some hardware—and I'm talking professional-grade stuff, not amateur-hour kind of shit, got it?"

Mo's eyes narrowed. "You got a lot of balls, asking me to give you a hand when you just burned my business to the ground."

"It could be worse," I reminded him.

He snorted. "Oh yeah? How's that?"

I set my E-14 combat knife gently on the table in front of me, its wicked edge gleaming even in the bar's dim light. I gave him a broad smile, and the color drained from his face.

"Fine, but you've never met me, never heard of me, remember?" He wrote a phone number and address on a napkin. "Again, so you don't forget: you don't know me, don't even recognize my name, and you certainly didn't get this info from me, and you definitely don't know where I am or might be going, got it? Like… forever." He slid the napkin across the table at me and stood.

"See you in the afterlife, then?" I joked.

"I sure as hell hope not," he muttered as he left. Outside the bar, he hailed a passing cab and disappeared.

CHAPTER SIX

I finished my beer—a pretty shitty pilsner made locally—then asked the bartender where the restroom was. Once I'd taken a piss, I waited until the coast was clear, then ducked into the cramped, dirty kitchen and out the bar's back door. I don't have many principles, but one I do have is never paying for bad beer.

Outside, I flagged down a cab, paid with cash, and got dropped off two rings away from my destination. It was getting late and I was nearly exhausted, so I ducked into a seedy hotel situated on the cross section between H and I rings, and checked in without a name, since all the proprietor wanted was cash. Unfortunately for me, a quick look into the hidden pocket of my duffel where I kept my money revealed it was coming to an end. There was less than 600 credits left. That was going to put me pretty short when it came to eating and finding a place to sleep, much less what I was going to need for the hardware I was after. I wondered just how much I'd spent on booze during my two-day bender and decided it was best not to think about it.

I took the room key from the guy at the desk, made my way up two flights of stairs, then down a filthy hallway strewn with spent Grand tabs and empty Z autoinjectors. That did little to help my mood. Even if I'd somehow managed to lose Section Six by dumping the basilisk card, there was no guarantee I wouldn't get murdered in my sleep by some tripped-out zedhead or a loopy idiot riding high on Grand. My only comfort was that by the looks of things, I was in the company of plenty of other folks who weren't exactly friends of local law enforcement, so there was little chance anybody would report me as suspicious to local Sec.

When I got to my filthy, windowless room, I bolted the door — since I no longer had any faith in electronic locks — and tried to push the steel-framed bed up against it. Of course, the ratty bed itself was welded to the floor.

I couldn't shake the idea that I was pretty damn likely to get killed during the night — the only question was by who. Pushing that thought out of my mind, I got down to business and used the room's graffiti-marked public terminal to call the number Mo had given me.

The screen displayed *Camera System Not Installed* instead of a picture, but at least someone answered.

"Yeah?" the voice on the other end said.

"I need some hardware, and a friend of mine said you might be able to help me out," I answered.

"Who the fuck gave you my number?"

I smiled. I knew how this game was played. "C'mon, man, you think I'm that dumb? You could be local Sec for all I know, or some UNF task force. Fuck that! I meet you at the address he told me and we talk there—nothing else tonight. All right?" I'd dealt with suspicious lowlifes my entire life and was pretty much a suspicious lowlife myself, so I knew that nothing eased the paranoia of one party in a two-party deal like equal paranoia on the part of the other party.

"Fine," the man on the other end said. "You show up at the right place tomorrow—ten hundred local—and we'll see if I can help, all right? Bring it liquid and clean or else you get nothing, okay?" *Cash on hand, no traceable payment.*

"Yeah, I copy."

"Good." The terminal beeped and an *End Call* message flashed onscreen.

I cut off the light and dragged the piss-stained, sheetless mattress off the bed frame and onto the floor in front of the door. The way I figured, if Section Six came for me in the middle of the night, they'd expect me to be in the bed, which meant that was the last place I wanted to be. I laid my head closest to the door and tried to block out how bad the mattress smelled — or was that my own odor? — and cursed the fact that the hall light shone through the large crack underneath the room's fiberglass door. I lit a cigarette and didn't expect to get a whole lot of shuteye.

I must have fallen asleep anyway, because I was awakened by a muted voice and the shadows of feet in front of my door. I went from a dead sleep to hyper-alert in an instant, my heart pounding a million beats a minute like an out of control drum machine. All I could see through the gap between the door and the floor was a pair of nondescript black shoes in decent condition — shoes too nice to belong to a long-term inhabitant of this shithole. Whoever was outside my door whispered something so softly I couldn't make it out.

My mind raced — local cops? A random Insys drug raid? Section Six? Had Rise somehow tracked me down from yesterday's intrusion into their hangar bay? Somebody I'd pissed off and didn't even remember from the two days I'd blacked out?

It was probably a bad sign that I needed a cross-referenced, indexed file system to keep track of everybody who had it out for me.

The pair of shoes took a step back, and I noticed a detail that answered my questions in the worst possible way.

One of the shoe bottoms was covered in a very distinctive metallic green paint.

Jade's warning to me the previous day echoed in my head, and my blood froze in my veins. I was looking at a member of Section Six, probably one who'd been tracking me ever since they released me into the wild three days ago.

I unsheathed my knife and stood as quietly as I could. I risked a look out the door's peephole and saw a plain-looking, dark-haired man dressed like the perfect picture of one of Bohr's cab drivers—dirty gray sweatpants, blue T-shirt, and faded brown jacket. The license clipped to his coat collar had a valid union sticker and even sported the normal, telltale scuffs on the left side from being run through the ring strip-readers. If I hadn't seen the paint on his shoe, I never would have given him a second look.

The Section Six goon whispered something else, probably to a throat mic or an implant I couldn't see. Whatever the response was, it made him roll his eyes. Through the peephole, I read his lips to clearly make out the last word of his transmission — *roger*.

I watched in horror as he fished one of the basilisk cards out of his left coat pocket and a sleek black pistol from his right. I didn't have to be a fortune-teller to know what was coming next.

This motherfucker was coming in.

He had me trapped like a rat. There was no way out of the room but the door he was getting ready to come through, and there was nowhere to hide. Hell, my shitty little hotel room didn't even have a bathroom. Meanwhile, the only weapon I had was a knife, while he was toting what I recognized was a brand-new UNF-issue Stieger antimatter pistol — meaning if he couldn't get the door open, it would only take two shots from that pistol to open up a hole big enough for him to walk through in the door *or* the wall, his choice.

My life is a series of impossibly shitty circumstances.

He waved the basilisk card in front of the door, and I heard a quiet *click* as the electronic lock disengaged. The claw-style door handle twisted slowly as he tried to let himself in, but the deadbolt held it in place. He took a step back and readied himself to kick his way in.

I had a sudden flash of inspiration that bordered on lunacy, but I'd seen it done in a few shitty holos before, so I tried it. I slid the mattress away with my foot and unbolted the door just as he lifted his leg. Then, I snatched the door wide open just as his foot would have made contact with it.

In what was a total and complete surprise to me, the trick actually worked.

Expecting the door to provide resistance, he'd thrown his weight behind his kicking leg, which meant he fell right through the doorframe and stumbled forward into the dark room. I brought my knife down into the side of his neck, figuring he was probably wearing a protective vest underneath his cab driver's uniform.

The blade sank in to the hilt, and he collapsed to the floor. I followed, keeping pressure on the knife handle. We wound up in a heap on the mattress with my hand clamped over his mouth to stifle his scream. He gasped once, kicked a few times, then didn't move again. I pushed the door closed and scrambled off of him, adrenaline surging and my heart thudding so hard I felt like it would beat out of my chest. Once I got my breath, I switched on the light to look at what I'd done.

The Section Six agent lay face up on the mattress, bright red blood pooling under him from the wound in his neck as his dead eyes stared at the ceiling. It took me a pull or two, but I got the blade out of him and wiped it clean on the mattress before

I resheathed it. I wondered if the hotel would bother replacing the mattress or if they'd just flip it over for the next guest.

The dead man's hand still held his pistol, which I gingerly retrieved. I inspected it to see if it was tied to biometrics or needed a badge to function. Fortunately, the pistol didn't have so much as a serial number, much less anything electronic that would allow it to be traced. I checked the magazine and found it full: twenty-five shots. I wrestled his brown jacket off him and retrieved two more full pistol mags along with a huge wad of cash from an inner pocket. As I counted it, I couldn't keep the grin off my face—there was almost twenty large in all.

But a pistol and a bunch of cash wasn't the only thing useful I found. Untucking his shirt from his pants confirmed my earlier hunch about a vest, which I managed to get off the corpse. I couldn't identify the make, but if it was Section Six kit, it had to be good.

After a lot of effort and more blood on my hands than I'd intended, I relieved him of his vest and put it on. It was a little big at first, but whatever nanotech it was made of compressed itself around me in a few seconds. By the time I put my T-shirt back on, the vest's outline was hardly visible. I threw on his jacket after I searched every inch of it for trace tags, tucking the cash and pistol back into its pockets.

With that, I slung my duffel bag over my shoulder and left the body for the roach-motel staff to deal with.

On my way out, I noticed his black basilisk keycard had landed outside the room. Walking two doors down the ratty hallway, I used the card to open the door and walked in on two naked Z heads about to get it on.

They made a move to stand, but thought better of it when I pulled the pistol out of my jacket pocket. They sank back down onto their mattress.

"Yo, listen up," I told the pair as I held the basilisk card up between two fingers. "This card will open anything electronic—*anything*. I don't need it anymore, so it's yours, aight? Now go score some of the good shit." I flicked it across the room to them and walked out.

I chuckled as I made my way down the hotel's fire escape, picturing Section Six following two Z fiends on a drug-fueled crime spree across Bohr Station while trying to get their card back without gunning down anyone in broad daylight or having to explain themselves to the local cops.

Back in the street, I found the orange and white cab whose number matched the agent's license. An idea struck me, and I opened the trunk. After a bit of rummaging around, I found what I was looking for—the safety kit. I pulled out the road flare and threw the rest of the kit back in the trunk. The magnetic strip on the license let me in the driver's door, where I pulled up the navigation screen, selected the *Return to Previous Destination* option, and cracked the driver's window a few centimeters. I tossed the license in the driver's seat, followed by the lit road flare.

Surprise, motherfuckers.

I slammed the door and stepped away from the curb, thick black smoke already curling from the open window. The electric motor spooled up, and the cab pulled away, headed back to wherever the agent had come from. As I watched it go, I lit a cigarette and sighed. The best I could hope for was to cause TPM a little chaos—that way, when he caught and killed me I could go out knowing I'd caused him at least some minor level of inconvenience.

When you're at the bottom, it's best not to set your sights too high.

CHAPTER SEVEN

After a quick breakfast from a vending machine and a visit to a pay shower where I spent a nerve-racking five minutes trying to clean my ass with a bar of soap in one hand and a pistol in the other without shooting my dick off, I made my way over to the address Mo had given me. The place turned out to be a ground floor unit in a block of apartments on the D ring in what looked to be a pretty decent part of the station.

I checked my watch and verified that I was within five minutes of the ten hundred hit time I'd been given. In this sort of transaction, it's not good to be too early, but then again, you also don't want to be late.

A security gate prevented me from getting into the building, but I buzzed the apartment Mo had listed.

"Yeah?" the same voice from last night answered.

"It's me—from last night," I told him. "You said to be here at ten hundred, and here I am."

"Alone?" he grunted.

"Yeah, man, more than I'd like to be, you catch me?"

The voice on the other end snorted. "Oh yeah? Well, I ain't in the girl business, got it? So I hope that ain't the kind of hardware you're looking for. I'll let you in."

The gate unlocked, and I followed the hallway to the apartment. There was a flash behind the peephole, and then the door opened.

A rough-looking guy in an expensive tracksuit opened the door halfway. It didn't take a genius to figure out that he probably had a pistol trained on me with the hand I couldn't see.

"You hot?" he asked.

"Yep," I told him as I slowly pointed to the right coat pocket. "Got a Stieger I sketched off a UNF buddy of mine, but it's clean."

"A Stieger, eh? Good piece. Come on in."

I followed him into a clean, well-furnished apartment. He closed the door behind me but never turned his back to me. His other hand remained in his tracksuit pocket and never left. I got the message: *no sudden moves.*

"Take a load off," he said and gestured to a spot on the couch. He settled into a chair across from me.

I set my duffel bag on the floor and took a seat. "All right," he said after he'd studied me for a second. "Whatcha looking for?"

"Okay, first, a coupla things," I told him. "This is a one-time buy—and I'm the principal, okay, so what you see is what you get. Don't fuck around with me thinking you'll get leverage with him, 'cause I'm him, and you won't. I'm it. Second, I'm in a bit of a time crunch, so I don't have a lot of time to be bullshitting over terms and whatnot, which is good news for you. Now, I've got the green to pay for it, too, so I'm not gonna try to rip you—but don't take that as a go-ahead to try and sketch me, got it?"

"Just tell me what you're looking for," the man said with a sly smile. "And I'll tell you what you'll pay if you want to get it."

I shrugged. "Fine. I need something that can hit hard—my targets are gonna be kitted up—and at a decent distance. And I'm talking about personal weapons, not heavy ordinance, okay? I'm trying to keep somebody safe, not start a war, got it?"

"I got it," he said. "You said you need it quick—how quick?"

"Today. Definitely today," I answered. "Oh yeah, and one other thing—I got to fit it in my duffel bag. I'm, uh, kinda in between housing at the moment, so I don't really have anywhere to stash it."

"I get you, man. If you need it today, that gives us four options—I can get you a Parker MP7 Laz if—"

"Can't take anything laz, unfortunately. I wish I could, but my ship's impounded, so I got nowhere I can plug it up. Unless you're selling it to me charged."

"Ha. No."

"So that's out."

I really wished I could have gotten a lazgun, as nothing could beat them for power and accuracy, but without the ship, there was nowhere I could find a convenient high voltage utility hookup and let it sit for four hours while the capacitors charged.

"Okay, so nothing laz," the arms dealer said with a shrug. "That leaves two other options. First, I got a UNF standard LR401. The underbarrel grenade launcher is an A model, but a lot of guys prefer that to the C model anyway. Second, if you don't need quite that much range, I got a fully tricked-out Schenzen ACP—laser mic scope, night vision, the whole kit."

"Is the ACP that submachine gun/rifle hybrid came out a few years ago? Bullpup design, super accurate to half a klick, high-velocity smart rounds, all that good stuff?"

"Yeah, that's it. If you want it, you got it and five hundred rounds for ten k."

"Ten grand? You want ten thousand credits for that thing?" I exploded. "That thing sells legit for like three-and-a-half k!"

He shrugged. "So go buy it legit, then."

"Real fucking funny. But listen, even if I give you double the markup for you covering, you're fucking me over big time!"

"Ten k. Take it or don't, I don't care, but if you need it now, and you need it bad, that's what it costs."

I shook my head. "Seven grand is as high as I go."

"Eight and a half and it's yours." He gave me a faux-smile, and I sighed. Realistically, there wasn't much I could do, even if I wasn't thrilled about forking over so much of the only money I had.

"Fine, and that thing better come clean, never-fired, and in a case, too, for that price."

My contact snapped his fingers. A short brunette woman, who prior to this point I had no idea was even there, appeared from an adjoining room.

"KP, get one of the ACPs for him — case too — and five hundred rounds," the arms dealer said. She nodded and returned a minute later with a hard plastic, olive-drab weapon case and a metal box with *UNF RESTRICTED USE ONLY* stamped on the side.

I took the case first, snapped it open, and inspected its contents. The camouflaged assault rifle measured only half a meter in length with its folding stock collapsed, its vented seven-millimeter barrel poking out from underneath a tan plastic hood that reminded me of a cobra's head. Foam cutouts in the case held the weapon's scope and vision enhancement package, a silencer, and several other accessories I wasn't familiar with.

I nodded. Now *this* would even the score a bit.

I closed the box lid and had a look at the ammo can. The smart rounds were still in their original packaging, and the UNF shipping seal was unbroken. I still knew I was getting taken, but at least I was getting good product.

"All right, I'll take it." I unfolded my wad of money which raised some eyebrows, but the weapons dealer counted and took my eight-and-a-half grand without comment.

After stuffing everything into my duffel bag, I found myself back outside the apartment—my bankroll a lot lighter, my bag a lot heavier, and without a clue as to what to do next. All I knew was that if I didn't get to Carla before the boss and The Pale Man, all the firepower in the world wasn't going to help.

I didn't know where I was going, but at least I had the tools to fuck somebody up when I got there.

CHAPTER EIGHT

I took the train back up to M deck and around to block five again to check out Rise's hangar deck and see if I could figure out an approach besides blasting my way in like some sort of action movie hero, since I knew that—unlike in the movies—that approach was probably going to end with me taking a ten-millimeter slug to the face. I scowled just thinking about the boss's stupidity that had cost me my best chance to get in earlier.

What I saw when I actually got to block six was even worse than I'd expected. Where there had been two Rise enforcers before, there were now four, and a roving patrol of three gang members on top of that. The whole of block six was locked down tighter than hell's gates, meaning my chances of getting inside to warn Carla, if she was even there in the first place, were reduced from minimal to absolute zero.

Cursing under my breath, I grabbed a snack from a vending machine, then got back on the maglev, intending to ride for a few more hours and then come back to see if things had calmed down. I stretched across two seats and closed my eyes for a minute, trying not to dream of Carla.

A godawful racket that sounded like two metal cats fucking in a trashcan woke me up.

I opened my eyes to a train car full of bare-foot passengers dressed in flowing robes in garish colors ranging from incandescent orange to seizure-inducing patterns in blue and red. Apparently not content to assault everybody's eyes by dressing like technicolor LSD vomit, the crowd banged on tambourines, clinked finger cymbals, rang necklaces of bells, and clapped to a rhythm only they could discern. The group swirled around to what I guessed was supposed to be music, even if to me it had all the organization and beauty of a rockslide wiping out a remote mountain village.

I scowled. *Rais*, converts to the worship of Rai, a "prophet" of some vague and indeterminate sort. The guy had been dead for forty years or so after some poor ex-member of his cult had blown up his shuttle in Vola somewhere once he'd discovered the exalted Rai had been banging his wife. Even so, Rai's followers still flew around in large flotillas from planet to planet and station to station, picking up converts, handing out flowers, and generally mucking about making noise. They were pretty harmless as a rule—in fact, in my earlier years, I'd eagerly awaited the arrival of the Rais to whatever rock I was currently marooned on, as they were pretty big on "conversion through love" and the Rais girls were usually a damn sight better looking and more willing than the locals.

They sang something in a language I didn't recognize and then again in common: "Long live Rai's Eternal and Glorious Kingdom, reflection of the beauty of Rai's Eternal Deathless and Spotless Soul." The crowd swirled around, banging their tambourines and making a racket that made me want to put a gun to my head.

"Will you shut the fuck—" I tried to say but was drowned out by another shouted chant.

"Glory to Rai's—Glory to Rai's—Glory to Rai's—" the women shouted.

"—Eternal and Glorious Kingdom!" the men called in response.

"Just st—" I began before I stopped mid-word. I listened to their chant again.

"Glory to Rai's—Glory to Rai's—"

I remembered Jade saying Carla was working for Rise, but a question hit me like a shot of Z—*what if Carla wasn't working for Rise, but for the Rais?*

I grabbed the nearest man by the folds of his green robe. "Shut the hell up for a second and listen to me," I snarled at him. "How long have you guys been on Bohr? When did you show up? Do you guys have private security traveling with you?"

He danced away without answering, but a dark-haired beauty appeared out of the whirling crowd and put a soft hand on my shoulder. "Brother, do you wish to learn about joining into the Oneness of the Universal Rai?"

"Look, sister, if what I'm working on doesn't work out, you can talk to me about Oneness anytime, okay? But the thing is, right now I'm kinda on my own personal—uh—quest for, uh, enlightenment or whatever, okay? Kinda my own *journey of discovery*, you might say—and what I really need is some actual, no-shit, concrete info from you guys."

She gave me a disappointed pout at first, then smiled. "Okay, brother, whatever you say."

I was reminded of something Jade had said about eye-fucking girls when I was supposed to be on a noble quest and did my best to keep my mind firmly on Carla.

"I'm looking for somebody who might be traveling with you guys, all right? And I need to find her. She's in a lot of danger. If I—"

The Rai woman cut me off. "No one is in danger if they travel in the Oneness of the Rai, searcher," she told me. "His Deathless and Spotless Soul protects us all in spirit and —"

"Yeah, okay, fine," I interrupted. "But the thing is she isn't a Rai, okay? She's security — muscle — the one protecting your definitely *not* deathless bodies. And she's in some deep shit and doesn't even know it, so if one of you could help me find her instead of trying to convert me and all that jazz, I'd really appreciate it — might make me more likely to join up later, right?" I added helpfully, if completely untruthfully.

An older Rai who'd been listening in on our conversation spoke up. "She is trying to show you the Way, searcher," he told me gravely. "But because the Rai was compassionate and loving, so shall we be. The Pilgrimage vessels are docked on D deck — all of blocks two and three."

I reflected on that bit of information. The Rais/Rise angle was a bit of a longshot, admittedly, but it was definitely worth checking out — the Rais were much less likely to blast me into gibbets just for poking around their docking bay.

"I work communications on the *Glorious Prize*," the old man explained. "And we have four escorts with the pilgrimage. They're all docked inside the

Flower of the Soul. Two fighters, a heavy corvette, and a single-seat combat shuttle I thi—"

My heart leapt in my chest. "A combat shuttle? Single seat, you said? What kind? Was it a Razor?" While Razors weren't the rarest ships in the sector, they weren't very common either, and I'd never known Carla to fly anything else.

The old man shook his head and smiled. "Searcher, I couldn't tell you what kind. I never paid attention, but I hope it is, for your sake. Maybe then you will find what you look for—and afterward, what you *need*."

"Yeah, sure, man," I told him. "Thanks, though—seriously," I added. I felt I should say something else, but expressions of gratitude aren't really my area of expertise. The train slowed as it approached a node station.

Just before I slipped through the maglev's sliding doors, I nodded to the crowd of Rais. "May the Force be with you or… whatever."

The old man laughed. "Searcher, someday, I hope you find the light of the Rai."

The doors closed and the train sped on its way, taking its noisy, tambourine-beating Rais with it.

———————————————-·

From the node station, I took a different maglev up to D deck and the pilgrimage blocks. The place was a sea of colors and noise—between the singing, shouting, dancing Rais and the curious visitors from the rest of Bohr, it was only a few decibels shy of deafening. There were flowers everywhere, food being cooked in open stalls, shouted classes on enlightenment to any poor station resident unfortunate enough to stop within earshot of a Rai, and what appeared to be a small but vocal counterprotest given by some of the station's other more traditional religions.

The crowd dashed any hope I had of quickly finding Carla among the Rais—even if she were somewhere in the mass of humanity that was the pilgrimage blocks, how the hell was I going to find her? I could barely even see over the edge of the crowd, much less closer to the ships where she was likely to be hanging out. I knew Carla well enough to know that while she'd take their money, she wasn't about to set off on some "journey of enlightenment" with a bunch of flower-print-wearing, manic-dancing, street-preaching loonies like the Rais, and although I'd never asked her opinion on unsolicited tambourine accompaniment, I was pretty sure she was no more thrilled with it than I was.

In fact, I reflected, she was unlikely to be outside the ships at all. It was far more probable that she was staying onboard whatever large Rai ship her Razor was docked on, drinking and doing whatever she did to pass the time. I tried not to think about what the boss had said about what Carla got up to when I wasn't around.

As I puzzled over what to do, I noticed a crew from one of the in-sector networks moving lights and holo rigs from a van to an open maintenance access door set into one of the station's massive internal structural ribs. I followed the rib upward toward where it curved into the bulkhead of C level, craning my neck to see what was going on. I gathered a set of stairs or ladders must have run up the rib, because at the top several other doors opened to maintenance catwalks that overlooked the docking bays. A pair of technicians stood on the lowest catwalk, installing a light set to better illuminate the scene for filming.

I tightened my duffel bag on my shoulders, parked myself close to the network van, and waited for my chance.

When a technician dragged a black lightbox out of the van, I grabbed a heavy reel of fiber optic cable and fell in behind him. Another network employee walked past me toward the van and didn't give me a second look. I followed the first tech into the rib until I met a guy with a clipboard. He checked his notes and gave me the once-over.

"That the forty-five a or the forty-five b?" he asked.

I looked down at the cable reel. Stenciled across the top was *047*.

"Neither. It's the forty-seven," I said.

He looked down at his clipboard. "Huh. Okay. They asked for the forty-fives next, but they'll have to have that forty-seven up there eventually anyway. Take it up to the first catwalk and tell Hakim to go ahead and run this to the retrans, and we'll send one of the forty-fives up next, all right?"

"Sure thing," I answered as I ascended the cramped metal stairs.

My legs were killing me by the time I reached the first catwalk, and I gladly dropped the spool of cable off with Hakim. When he turned to start his work, I trudged up the stairs instead of back down them, climbing all the way to the top landing. Once there, I opened up the door and let myself out onto the catwalk.

The scene below was no less chaotic from a distance. In fact, my height two hundred meters above it only made things worse. I wasn't prone to vertigo generally, but between my aching legs, the roar of noise, swirling color, and the height, I felt a little light-headed. I scowled as I slipped my duffel bag off my back and slumped down to the metal grating and pulled the rifle case out of my bag. I opened it and stared down at the ACP and its various components.

Before I set to work, I took a quick glance around, just to make sure no one else had decided to come up here with me, because I knew I pretty much fit the exact profile of every holofilm crazy I'd ever seen. I mean, how much more stereotypical can you get than the lone gunman on the catwalk with a rifle? The last thing I needed was for some johnny-do-gooder to pitch me right off the side of the catwalk to the deck two hundred meters below, with him thinking he's doing a good deed for society when really all he's doing is being an interfering sonofabitch.

I assembled the ACP, screwed on the silencer, and attached the laser mic scope to the accessory rail atop the rifle, but didn't bother with the earbuds. I wanted to see, not hear. I flicked on the scope's enhancement switch and laid prone on the uncomfortable catwalk.

From my perch, I scanned across the crowd with the patience of a predatory animal. Back to front, diagonal across the middle of the crowd, then front to back, working my way over the scene in a *z* pattern. I examined every face I could, looking for

Carla or anybody who I thought might be one of Section Six's assassins.

After I'd been scanning for a few minutes and was just about to pull back from the scope to take a break, a familiar black jacket caught my eye. At what my scope told me was a range of 362.4 meters, there was my former boss trying to fight his way through the crowd.

I muttered a list of dubious claims about his ancestry, disparaging remarks about his sexual ineptitude, and generally every insult I'd ever heard plus a few I'd come up with on the spot as I watched him navigate his way through the kaleidoscope of Rais.

He reached a line of the cultists dressed all in red. That bunch seemed to serve as gatekeepers to a relatively empty section of the crowded deck that looked like it was reserved for meetings or planning sessions. Behind them, a handful more Rais pored over documents laid out on the tables. I figured it must have been a place for pilgrimage leadership to discuss things—why they didn't stay on the ship to do so, I couldn't imagine—but looking for logic with the Rais was a bit of a fool's errand.

The boss said something to one of the red-dressed Rais, and the man nodded, then allowed him through the cordon. I fumbled around for the earbuds I hadn't plugged in earlier. I turned on the laser mic, hoping to figure out what the hell the boss was doing—and how he'd gotten admittance to what appeared to be the Rai inner circle.

He took a nervous glance over his shoulder into the teeming throngs of people behind him, and I wondered just who he was scared of. If he was going to give Carla to The Pale Man, what did he care if he was being followed?

He made his way to an empty table and took a seat facing the crowd, which put his back to the Rais' docked ships. Through the scope, I could make out sweat beading on his forehead and watched his eyes flick from face to face in the mass of people around him.

"What are you so nervous about, you son of a bitch?" I whispered as I kept the crosshairs on his chest. "You're the one who's doing what The Pale Man wants you to. It's me who should be nervous."

My heart leapt as Carla appeared from the outer edge of the scope, wearing brown mechanic's coveralls covered in grease, her hair dyed purple. She smiled at my former boss. He looked relieved.

"How the hell did you know I was on Bohr?" she asked as she walked toward him. "And where's Snake?" Her voice sounded tinny and electronic over the laser mic. "I got your message, but—"

"Snake is in trouble, Carla. Big time," he interrupted. "I don't know where he is. We—"

"Where is he? What kind of trouble? When did you see him last? The police? Or somebody else?" Carla barked questions too fast for him to answer, concern evident in her voice even through the distortion of the scope-mic. "Is he hurt? Did he—"

"Listen to me. Somebody crazy is looking for you, Carla—crazy like you can't imagine. He grabbed us both and told us we had to find you because he couldn't. And then Snake got gone, and I—"

"What kind of crazy somebody?" she interrupted, turning pale.

I could tell from the boss's face that he wasn't sure how much he wanted to say. "Do you know Section Six—like, the *person*?"

Carla's eyes widened. "Oh God, no. Nonononono... He's dead. I killed him."

The boss seemed relieved he wouldn't have to explain further. "'Fraid not, Carla. He's still alive, and he wants you bad. He sent me and Snake after you and..." He trailed off, and I saw a shadow of guilt cross his face. "And... and, we, uh, had a... uh... disagreement and got separated and so—"

Carla's eyes narrowed. "A disagreement? Over what?"

My finger tightened on the trigger. *It's truth or die time, boss.*

He looked away before he answered. "He didn't want to turn you over to the guy, and I… I know it seems bad, now, but I didn't think we had a choice, so I said that we should —"

"And you think you're gonna take me in, dumbass?" Carla spat. "I will chew you up and shit you out, so —"

"I'm sorry, okay?" the boss exploded. "I'm sorry! Look, I'm just trying to find Snake because these guys are gonna kill him if they figure out he isn't going to do what he's supposed to. I'm not gonna try to turn you in. I'm just trying to protect Snake from his own stupidity, okay?"

Carla crossed her arms in front of her. "Good call, flyboy. Now, where is he? 'Cause if anything has happened to him, I swear to fucking God you will wish you were dead."

I smiled from my position on the catwalk.

"Last I saw him we were on M deck, in Rise's docking bay and —"

"When?"

A shouted commotion from the mass of Rais drowned his answer. I pulled my eye off the scope and looked down just in time to see four figures, pistols out, emerge from the crowd. They wore colorful saris like Rais, but their speed and the way they held their weapons with practiced familiarity told me they were professional gunhands.

Two explosions thundered from the mass of people below. My ears rang and a jarring shockwave jolted up through the catwalk. One of the four assailants threw something cylindrical into a knot of Rais that approached them. I recognized it as a stun grenade just before it went off and left a half-dozen Rais gasping on the deck or staggering away. The rest of the crowd stampeded away from the raised platform, screaming and shouting. The four armed assailants quickly dispatched the line of red-dressed Rais with a combination of stun guns and jujitsu.

I winced and shook my head to clear it, trying to get a bead on somebody—anybody.

Gunshots in quick succession drew my attention back to Carla. She and the boss crouched behind an overturned table, smoking pistols in hand, but aside from making the Section Six agents duck behind tables of their own, the gunfire had little effect.

"Give her to us!" one of the Section Six goons shouted.

"Fuck you, motherfuckers!" Carla shouted. "He isn't giving you *shit*. You want a piece of me, you're gonna have to come take it."

The boss didn't answer, instead squeezing off two more shots that went wide but at least kept the attackers' heads down.

I ducked back down behind the scope in time to hear Carla taunt them again. "I already killed that rat bastard Zander once, and I will absolutely do it again, and you along with him, you hear me?" She got off a few shots of her own, one of which caught an agent as he darted to a closer table, but the round ricocheted off his personal shielding system.

One of the agents who was crouched behind an overturned table pulled a stun grenade from a vest under his sari. I swung the crosshairs to him and took a breath.

Through the scope mic I heard him mutter something I couldn't make out. I shot him just as he pulled the pin and stood to toss it.

The recoil was nowhere near as bad as I'd expected, and the silencer muffled the shot to a low *thump*. His personal shielding system flashed white as the high-powered round zipped through it and hit him in the middle of his back. The agent jerked forward, then toppled backward, his stun grenade rolling away from his outstretched hand.

The grenade exploded with a *whump* that startled the other three agents. I put the crosshairs on the agent farthest from the grenade. He looked like he was getting ready to bolt from behind his concealment toward the boss and Carla. He was going to pay for that.

Another *thump* and shield flash, and his blood splattered across the deck as the round passed clean through him.

By now, the other two agents had realized something was up and had leapt to the other side of their tables. I guessed they figured they'd rather take their chances that their shields would stop Carla and the boss's pistols rather than expose themselves to whoever was hunting them with the big stuff.

I didn't care.

I flipped the selector switch on the side of my carbine to full auto and cut loose.

The weapon jumped and *thuuuuuummmmmppp*ed, but I held it steady enough to saw one table—and the agent behind it—in half before transitioning over and catching the final Section Six man with a half dozen rounds as he tried to clear the distance remaining between him and where the boss and Carla hunkered down.

The boss poked his head up over the table and looked at the carnage around him. He seemed confused, as normal.

"Yo, boss!" I shouted down from my catwalk. "Give that pistol to Carla nice and slow or else I got one for you too, asshole!"

"What?" he called back, looking around to see where I was. "I'm on your side, Snake, you dumb son of a bitch!"

I switched back to semi and put a round into the table a few centimeters from his neck. "What's that?" I yelled. "It's hard to hear you up here. And it's gonna be *real* hard to hear you when you don't have a head!"

The boss raised his middle finger from behind the table but handed his revolver to Carla.

"I'm coming down," I called. "But don't get comfortable, just in case there's more of them on the way."

I made my way down as quickly as I could and then across the now-empty bay. It seemed even the Rais who'd been hit by the stun grenades had managed to evacuate when the shooting started.

I reached Carla, expecting a hug and a long, deep kiss for having just ridden white-knight-style to the rescue, but I got no such thing. She stood with her arms crossed and a scowl on her face.

"What took you so long?" she snapped.

Say fucking *what*?

"Huh?" I asked. "What are you talking about? You aren't the easiest person to track down, you know. Besides, I got here as soon as this asshole," I finished as I pointed to the boss.

Much to my surprise, the boss grinned. "Like hell you did. I sent her a message via the senior Rai fleetmaster not three hours after you showed your ass in the bar and almost got yourself shot."

"Whoa, wait a minute," I sputtered. "You knew she was here and where she was the whole time and didn't tell me?"

"Yeah, that's right, dipshit, I did," he snapped. "When was I supposed to tell you? In front of Dr. Death from Section Six? Or while you had a knife to my throat? I couldn't even get a word through to you because you wouldn't even listen to a thing I had to say anyway." I heard him, but the wheels in my head were churning over something else.

"Okay, fine. Then what the hell were you doing in Rise's docking bay when you almost got us both killed?" I demanded.

"She hadn't answered me back yet, and Jade was kind of unclear about things, so I was just checking out all my options. You know, thinking things through and whatnot. You oughta try it sometime, Snake." His voice was a bit too smug for a man whose life I'd just saved and who, last I talked to him, had been trying to sell Carla to TPM.

I pointed my carbine at him. "Shut it."

"I told you I was working with the Rais last time we were together," Carla said, arms still crossed. "Maybe if you'd listen to me more often, you'd know these things. Flyboy here did, and I'm not even banging him." She gestured to the boss, then shook her head and sighed. "Men are all the same—you get what you want and your damn ears stop working."

I gritted my teeth. "Look, can we talk about how well I listen and whatever about our relationship some other time, without him around? You know, since he was planning to turn you in and all, remember?"

"I said I was sorry," the boss cut in. "Jesus, Snake, you act like you've never fucked anything up before—I found Carla, and notice I'm not running off to tell Section Six anything, okay? So ease up on the virtuous crusader shtick, aight? It doesn't suit you."

"Touching," Carla said dryly. "You'd almost think you two were the couple." The boss and I both opened our mouths to protest, but she silenced us with a raised hand. "Okay, now that I have your attention, it's time to let the adult talk. Section Six is not going to go away, and they'll be back here with local Sec pretty damn soon. You two follow me, shut the fuck up for a minute, and we'll get to a safe place to figure out what the hell we're gonna do."

The boss and I rolled our eyes, but it wasn't like we had a better plan. Besides, it seemed like Carla knew more about Section Six than we did.

"Oh, yeah, here you go," she added as she handed the boss his pistol. "You can keep this for the time being, but remember which direction to point it, all right? I get the feeling you're trying to pull one over on me and you're gonna see my bad side—my real bad side—and it isn't pretty."

We followed her a few steps before Mo's warning about the basilisk card came rushing back to me.

"Yo, bossman," I said. "Get rid of that black card they gave us because—"

"No shit, Snake," he snapped. "I dumped it an hour after they gave it to me. Who the fuck would be stupid enough to walk around with a sec card they gave us? Who knows what that thing does?"

I felt my face flush, but I couldn't very well ask the question I wanted to: *Then how in the world did you get into Rise's maintenance area?*

CHAPTER NINE

Five minutes later, we were in a Rai cargo truck, on autopilot and headed for a ring and deck we'd chosen at random. From what I could tell by checking the van's traffic cameras, there was a suspicious lack of Bohr Sec presence after a shooting left four people sprawled out in a cargo bay with a coupla dozen witnesses, but I guess TPM had local sec under his pale, clammy thumb. Carla and I sat across from the boss. She reclined against me, which I took as a good sign.

"All right, Carla," the boss began. "Explanation time. Who the hell is this crazy asshole and why is he after us—after *you*, really—and what the hell are we going to do, since we're not gonna uh… ah… uh, give you up, I guess." I rolled my eyes. He was as smooth and thoughtful as ever.

As usual, Carla ignored the boss's casual boorishness. "That 'crazy asshole,' as you call him, is Alexander Corbin—he went by Zander back when I knew him. I doubt that's his real name, though—he lied about everything else, so why would his name be any different?"

"Well, even that's more than we had before," the boss replied. "But what the hell does he have to do with you?"

"He was—*is*—my ex-husband."

Carla said it so calmly and matter-of-factly that I almost fell off the bench.

There was a moment of awkward silence where the boss and I shared a look of bewildered horror. My mind raced. *Carla had slept with The Pale Man? Carla had been* married? *What the ever-loving fuck?*

The boss looked at me like he was waiting for me to say something, but I was still trying to piece everything together. "Uh, ah… Okay…" He cleared his throat. "Ahem, that's, uh, interesting, I guess, so—"

"What?" Carla interrupted. She turned to me, eyes ablaze. "Surely you didn't think I was some delicate flower waiting for your presence to blossom, did you?"

"N-Nooo," I said as evenly as I could. "It's just that… well… uh, I mean, have you *seen* that guy? I mean—"

Carla's eyes narrowed and then widened, as if she'd just gotten a joke. "What does he look like now?"

"Like a fucking nightmare, that's what," the boss replied. "Pale as a ghost, his eyes are oculars, and he's shiny bald—not even an eyebrow. And you married that dude?"

Carla gave a sharkish smile. "He didn't used to look that way—not back when I married him, anyway. The reason he looks like that now probably has something to do with why he's looking for me."

The boss's eyebrows went up. "Uh, what does that mean, exactly?"

Carla sighed and leaned back against me. "It's kind of a long story."

The boss and I looked at her expectantly.

She rolled her eyes. "Fine. Here goes, and no interrupting, or judging—especially not from your broke, lying, cheating asses, got it?"

"Deal," I said with a nod.

"I was working in a bar on Falschmir, years ago—just outta school. And *no,*" she said with a pointed glance at the boss, "I was not a 'working girl.' I was a drinky girl—you know, one of those good-looking girls who's way out of your league and comes up to you at the bar looking like a straight ten and gets you to buy her drinks all night long at ridiculous markups?"

I laughed as the boss turned red. "Oh, he knows the type, Carla." I nodded at the boss. "He attracts 'em like flies. It's like he's got 'sucker' in all-caps on his forehead. There was this one girl on Paris V, you shoulda—"

"All right, that's enough, asshole," the boss muttered. "Okay, so you were a drinky girl, I get it."

"So," Carla continued, "I was working at the club, and he showed up one night. Bought drinks like he owned the place, rolled with the big dogs, and there was something about him—I dunno exactly, but he exuded confidence and power, I guess." She shook her head. "You have to understand, at the time, I was just a poor girl with a fucked-up family situation and big dreams of getting off Falschmir and doing my own thing. I had no money, no connections, no nothing. And then here's Zander. He didn't even notice me at first—just another pretty face and nice ass in a club full of 'em—but eventually I got his attention and… the next time he came back, we just sort of chilled, you know?"

She grimaced at the memory before she continued. "He'd disappear for weeks at a time. He told me, sort of honestly, that he was in the UNF but couldn't really say what he did. I figured he was some sort of black ops heavy. I just didn't understand how heavy until later.

"Anyway, he started talking about taking me off Falschmir to a place he owned in New London or maybe a penthouse on Paris V. I'd met other guys who'd promised bullshit, but Zander was different—he had the power to actually do it." She frowned. "At the time, I was into powerful guys."

"I see you got over that," the boss noted.

"Shut up," I snapped.

"Eventually, we did leave. To New London. He had a penthouse there—A ring, two deck, the works. A week later, he proposes to me, and I was like 'who gets married nowadays?' but he sold me some line of romantic bullshit about how I was what he'd been looking for his whole life and all that stuff. Being nineteen and deep in love, I bought the whole thing, said yes, and three weeks later we were husband and wife, 'till death do us part,' and all that bullshit." She gave a pained smile. "Not too long after, he disappeared for coupla weeks and told me some people he knew from 'the Section' would be using the place for a bit. That's when I started to realize I was being played." She let out a long sigh.

"The crew was a rough bunch, which wasn't a surprise, but there was this one old guy—I never found out his real name, everybody just called him 'Control,' so I did too. Control was no saint, don't get it wrong—he was old-school covert ops from way back, probably before the Second Charter even. Anyway, I'm sure he had his skeletons, but he was actually pretty friendly to me, didn't treat me like shit like the rest of the guys did and kind of became almost the father I never really had."

"Ahhh," the boss said.

"Not too long after that, Zander came back for a day or two, then left again. He didn't tell me where he was going, just that he was on mission. Six months went by, but Control relayed messages from him. Never told me what he was up to, just that he was alive and 'thinking of me,' supposedly. Something about those messages seemed to bother the old man, but he wouldn't tell me what it was. Finally, I convinced myself that Zander must be dead and they just didn't want to tell me, so I holed up in my room crying for like two days before one of Zander's asshole buddies came by and made a pass at me.

"When I told him I was Zander's wife and to stay the fuck away from me, he just laughed like that was the biggest joke in the world and told me he and Zander had been together for a long while and that Zander never had a problem fucking any of his girls and he didn't expect Zander would have a problem with him fucking me—told me it'd happened before."

She paused and drew a breath. I looked down at her, thinking she might be crying, but I was wrong. The look on her face was not sadness, but fury.

"He then proceeded to tell me to get off my high horse and that if I thought I was anything special by calling myself Zander's 'wife' I needed to learn some things about the world. Then, he comes at me getting all grabby, but hey, I worked in a club, I can handle myself, right?

"Turns out, though, handling drunk university kids and handsy old men is a bit different than tangling with a professional heavy. Next thing I know, he's got me up against the wall, hand around my throat and is beating the shit out of me. Probably would have killed me if Control hadn't intervened.

"So Control sends everybody out of the room, and I'm in tears and all that mess and so he—probably against his better judgment—levels with me. He tells me what's been bothering him the whole time—namely, that Zander is about as trustworthy as… as… fuck, I dunno, but something not trustworthy, right? Zander really is covert ops, obviously, but other than that, he's been lying to me the whole time. The houses, the money, all that—cover shit, all taxpayer owned. Control tells me that even though I may be devoted to Zander, he's got girls all over the goddamned galaxy—and that in fact, Zander has actually been doing work on New London the whole time, and that, in addition to all that worrying I was doing while he was on the *same fucking station* I was, he was also banging one of his many other chicks.

"Ouch." I winced.

"Yeah. So I'm madder than hell at him and everybody else, and I start to try to throw them out—can you imagine me at twenty trying to throw out a bunch of spec-ops heavies? Yelling shit about 'get out of my house' when the place is owned by the goddamn UNF?" Carla sighed. "I hate—*fucking hate*—being helpless. I'd been that my whole life, and the whole reason I'd gone with Zander was so I wouldn't be helpless anymore. And there I was, worse off than when I started.

"So Control tells me he'll recall Zander and we can work it out, and he'll give us a bit of privacy. He clears everybody out but gives me a number and a location where I can find him later if we can't work it out, and tells me he'll set me up—since he kinda feels sorry for me. Earlier, I'd played up the pitiful girl angle and got one of the other guys who'd been checking me out for weeks to give me a pistol. I told him I needed it because when Zander threw me out I would need protection. I don't think it ever crossed his mind that I might actually do something else with it.

"I made Control promise not to tell Zander what was up, told him that I wanted to hear his lies myself—so when Zander showed up, he had no idea what I knew. I meet him in a black lacy number, acting like I've been waiting for him the whole time. He makes some vague references to being way out in Riker for months, acts like he's been in danger, tells me how he's thought about me the whole time and all that bullshit. He's such a natural born liar—a psychopath—that I almost believed it, and I knew better.

"So I lead him to the bedroom and tell him to lie down in bed. What he doesn't know is that I've already soaked the bed in porophol. As soon as he lies down, I knock a romantic candle I've got set up onto the bed and—*whoosh*."

I shuddered as the boss and I shared another look of horror. Carla, though, continued her story like it was the most normal thing in the world.

"Then, I run to the door—to the other side, I mean and—you two ever been to the upper decks in New London?"

"Huh? Uh, no," I stammered.

"Well, they've all got outward-facing windows, all the really nice places do, so you can look out and see Hygradia and Salseen—makes a nice view, really. Anyway, so from the other side of the door, I empty the pistol into the window and then all of a sudden *bang*, the window goes and out goes his screaming ass with it. Automatic atmosphere preservation kicks on, the bedroom door goes shut and sealed, and that's the last I saw of him. I figured he was dead."

She shrugged.

"I ran to Control and told him—kind of—what happened, and he mutters something about 'a woman scorned' but gives me a hefty bit of cash, the clean title to the Razor I'm still flying and—and this is most important—makes me into a kind of modern-day ghost. He told me I'd never find him again, or anybody else in 'the Section,' and not even to try. But he also promised he'd make sure nobody could find *me* either. He put some sort of irreversible track on my UNF master record and I disappeared. It's like I've got a valid ID, but the system refuses to log anything I do, anywhere I go. If you look me up, I don't exist—not even to the UNF, but yet I'm there, in the system—a whisper in the network, a shadow in the system. If you were to put my name into a database, anywhere, as soon as it touched a UNF network, I'd be gone, cleared out—you'd never know why, but it would happen. I knew some of the Section boys had been after me since then, but I figured it was revenge for killing Zander, not that it was Zander himself."

With that, she slumped back and slid even closer to me.

The boss spoke first. "So, somehow, he lived, and he's been... *hunting* you all these years? Of course, he can't find you because he can't even search for you or anything you've ever done. And now, basically, there's nothing he can't or won't do to find you, especially since he's got to know he's close... We are fucked, aren't we?"

"Control can stop him," Carla offered. "If we can find—"

"I don't think Control is around anymore," I interrupted. "From what TPM—uh, Zander—told us, there's only one founding member of Section Six anymore, and Zander is it. He talked about a former partner of his who died in a shuttle 'accident' and I think Control is who he was talking about."

A look of genuine sadness crossed Carla's face. "Zander killed him? Control was the only nice one out of any of them. Figures, that bastard."

There was something else on my mind though. I just couldn't shake the mental picture of TPM lying there, on fire in his bed, and then suddenly being explosively decompressed out into space.

Finally, I said it. "I just want you to know that, uh, since we've been together, I've never—"

The boss and Carla looked at me like I was an idiot.

"Snake, you're a dumbass," Carla said. "I don't care, and you know why?"

"'Cause he's not worth caring about?" the boss asked. We both ignored him.

"Because I'm not nineteen anymore. And for some reason, I knew with you, I'd be all right. I never knew if it would work out long term, but I know, somehow, that you'll do right by me. I know you actually care about what happens to me and you're not asking me to do something or be some way you aren't yourself. And when it ends, one of us will just say it's over and we'll be cool. I can respect that. I don't know how I know, but I do. Deep down, even though you don't know it, you're really a good guy, in the end."

I opened my mouth to say something but didn't know what. "Good guy" was not a term I'd heard used to describe me before. Ever. I closed my mouth and tried to think of something appropriate to say.

The boss's moment-ruining skills are the stuff of legend though. "Well, that's really something sweet there, Carla, but in the meantime, how are we gonna—"

Carla's pistol came up and met the boss between his eyes.

"You. Front of the truck, now."

"But, but—" the boss protested.

"Ten, nine, three, two—" she counted.

"Okay, okay, okay," he grumbled as he clambered through the door to the truck cab.

"Don't stop the truck or come back here till you hear us bang on the door," she shouted.

Our clothes were off before the door even closed.

CHAPTER TEN

Two hours later, the three of us sat around a back table in a bar on F Deck nursing whiskeys, Carla and I contented and the boss with a sour look on his face.

"Come on," I said. "What's the big deal? Why so unhappy?"

"I dunno, a couple of reasons come to mind," he snapped. "First off, while I'm glad you are so happy to be reunited, that doesn't solve our problem, does it? Zander—or whatever his real name is—is still out there, and unless we figure something out quick, we're still gonna be disappeared in a matter of days. And…" He trailed off and took another sip of whiskey.

"And?" Carla said with a raised eyebrow.

"*And* that door wasn't very thick. I could have gone the rest of my life without hearing you two."

"Aww," Carla said. "I'm so sorry. Does it remind you of your crippling loneliness? When this is all over, I'll loan you a few creds and take you over to Kitty's, on E ring, and you can choose any of the—"

"Damn it, I'm serious," he interrupted. "What the hell are we going to do? The world isn't suddenly fixed just because Snake's dumb ass finally found you. For all we know, Section Six is on the way over here right now."

The thought of The Pale Man's goons busting into the bar wiped the smile off my face.

The boss nodded. "Yeah, that's right. Welcome back to the real world, Snake. Snap out of your post-coital bliss for long enough to realize we're dead men walking."

"Fuck that noise," Carla said. "I killed him once. I can kill him again."

"Yeah, well, see if you can do a better job this time around," my partner muttered as he drained his glass.

Carla snorted. "I'm not the one over here whining like a bitch and all 'woe is me, the scary man said he's going to do bad things.' That'd be you."

"You know, I'd forgotten how much I disliked you," the boss mused. "Maybe I should have turned you in."

"It's not too late to try, flyboy," Carla said, an edge in her voice. "If you think you're up to it."

"Whoa, whoa, calm down. He didn't really mean it," I said with a glare at the boss. "He's just stupid. I'm sure what he meant was—"

"Actually, that might work," Carla interrupted.

"Huh? What might work?"

"The only way y'all are going to get out of this mess is to get close enough to Zander to stop him from deleting your records. And the only way that's going to happen is if you've got me. Now, they already know you aren't going to turn me in, Snake, because you've already blasted a couple of them to hell and gone, so—"

"Also stabbed one," I added with a shrug.

The boss's eyes widened. "Jesus."

"Right," Carla continued. "So obviously they're not going to buy you having a change of heart and dragging me back to Zander. But they might buy it from ace here, provided we can come up with a plausible enough story. And he can keep from saying anything stupid."

"Well, we're royally fucked then," I muttered into my whiskey glass.

The boss glared at me before he spoke. "Okay, fine, but what good does that do? Even assuming they think I'm there to give you to Section Six, they'll probably search me for weapons, and I don't see us overpowering the ninja goon death squad at close quarters."

"You get me close enough, and I'll think of something. If anything, I can play on Zander's sympathy," Carla said.

My eyebrows went up, and I shared a skeptical look with the boss before addressing Carla. "*Sympathy*? I know you know him better than we do, but *sympathy* did not seem to be in the cards the last time we talked to him."

"Yeah," agreed the boss. "Not even a little bit. Less sympathy and more… *sadism*."

Carla rolled her eyes. "I'm well aware of his deep mean streak, thanks, but I'm telling you, I can handle him."

I was unconvinced, to put it mildly. "How do you know he isn't going to put a bullet between your eyes as soon as he sees you? Or worse?"

"Simple," Carla replied. "If he wanted me dead, his goons would have done it when they saw me. They could have, pretty easily. They were throwing stun grenades, remember? They could have just as easily thrown frags or plasma thumpers and I'd be a pink mist or a charred husk. Zander wants to see me—to talk to me—for some reason. He doesn't want me dead."

"He doesn't want you dead *yet*, you mean," said the boss. "Because let me tell you, he wants you dead. Snake can back me up on that."

I nodded. "He's right, Carla. The only reason he doesn't want to kill you quickly is because he wants to kill you slowly. I mean, us two?" I gestured to the boss. "Sure, he'd just space us and be done with it, but I don't even want to think of what he's got in store for you."

"So what's the play then?" Carla demanded. "So far I'm the only one with ideas, and all you two want to do is sharpshoot. If you got a better idea, spill it."

"Look, all I'm saying is that I didn't track you down just to hand you over to The Pale Man. The whole point was to warn you, not give you to him," I said with a resigned sigh.

Carla's expression softened, and she flashed me a smile. "You know, Snake, you're cute when you're trying to be noble, even if you suck at it. But you've got it all wrong. You two are scared of him, but I'm not. Because he should be scared of *me*."

———————————

You ever tried telling a woman something when she's got her mind made up already?

It's fucking pointless.

They do what they want to do, and you just go along for the ride. So it was with us and Carla, whose incredibly risky scheme she insisted we execute.

I knelt in the passenger-side floorboard of a rented truck, parked in a maintenance alley in the shadow of a pair of housing blocks so as to give me a good view of the exchange point while keeping the truck hidden. My rifle rested in the open driver's-side window, trained on a sales kiosk where Carl and the boss waited for the exchange.

They milled around nervously, casting fleeting looks up and down the deserted ring streets and flinching every time the maglev zipped past. The boss had picked up the handset in a public comms terminal a half an hour ago and whispered to whatever or whoever was listening to everything on Bohr Station: "I have her. Sector two and three junction. E deck. Middle ring. Seventeen-thirty. I want my ship back and a hold full of clean money, you fucks. No more funny business."

The plan was for the boss and Carla to go with Section Six while I trailed in the rented truck with the firepower. That meant me keeping watch where I was with my ACP to make sure nothing bad happened when Section Six showed up. The boss wore the vest I'd taken off the Section Six agent at the roach motel, just in case. Carla had my knife taped to the small of her back because we knew they wouldn't believe it if the boss hadn't taken her pistol from her, but we hoped they'd overlook a well-hidden blade.

I checked my watch. It was 1742 and still there was no sign of Section Six.

"Where are they?" I muttered. I hate it when people don't show up to my ambushes on time. If I'm going to go through the trouble to lay a trap, my enemy should at least do me the courtesy of being punctual to spring it.

The boss and Carla's heads snapped around, and I pulled my eye off the scope to get a look at whatever drew their attention. A red TEEC Cardinal four door headed toward the kiosk, slowing as it drew near. My heart pounded. Go time.

As I trained my scope on the vehicle, the station lights went out, plunging us into cave-like darkness. The emergency lighting didn't engage, leaving me too blind to even find the night vision toggle switch on the unfamiliar scope.

Before I could manage the first muttered curse, a *bang bang* accompanied by two flashes lit up the kiosk like a strobe light. I heard the squeal of tires and the whine of the TEEC's electric motors at full speed before the lights flickered back to life.

The TEEC sped away toward the outer ring as I scrambled into the driver's seat and punched the truck into drive, peeling out of the maintenance alley. My heart raced and my head swam.

Shit shit shit shit.

Carla was nowhere to be seen, and my boss lay on his back next to the kiosk.

———————————————

As I swerved toward the kiosk, intent on following the rapidly escaping red sedan, the boss sat up, rubbing his chest. I slowed just enough for him to yank open the passenger door, then accelerated so quickly he almost didn't make it into the cab.

"Fuck!" I roared as I pounded a fist on the truck's dash. "Fuck fuck fuck *fuck!*"

"They tried to stamp me," the boss wheezed as he massaged his chest. "The motherfuckers *shot* me!"

I nodded as I tried to keep the TEEC in view ahead. The truck's tires howled, and the electric motor readout displayed "maximum power" on the windshield heads-up display.

"I hate it when people double-cross us before we get the chance to do it to them," he muttered, wincing and feeling his chest as if he couldn't believe he wasn't leaking blood.

"That son of a bitch got Carla!" I shouted. "They got her, man! What the fuck happened?"

"You saw it, Snake. The car pulled up, lights went out, *bang bang*, I was shot and on my ass, and then they were gone. It was so fast I didn't have time to do shit."

I wanted to be mad at him, but there really wasn't much I could say. They'd been too quick for me as well, and had he not taken my vest, he'd have a pair of fist-sized holes in him. Plus, there isn't really much more you can ask of a guy than to take a pair of bullets for your girlfriend.

The red car ahead veered sharply right before it returned to its lane in a maneuver that told me it had to have been executed by computer-aided autopilot. It swerved again, this time to the left, before it slowed and returned to its lane.

"What the hell?" the boss asked.

"I don't—" I started to say before the rear driver's-side gullwing door opened and a body in a black suit tumbled out. The door closed.

The man bounced twice before he came to rest on the station deck. Transfixed as I was, I didn't even think to avoid him, but the truck did, swerving to avoid running him over. The red TEEC pulled off into a maintenance lane and slowed to a halt.

I hit the brakes and screeched up behind it. The boss and I were out, guns at the ready, before the truck even came to a stop.

The driver's gullwing door opened to reveal a grinning Carla, my bloody E14 combat knife to the throat of the driver, who by the look of pain on his face had already felt the bite of the black diamondite steel at least once.

My mouth dropped open.

"I told you, I can handle myself," Carla said by way of explanation. She winked.

The rear doors opened next. The stylish tan interior of the car looked like a low-budget horror holo—the seats slashed and blood everywhere.

"Jesus Christ," the boss said.

"It got a little messy," Carla said with a shrug. "But it's going to get even messier unless henchman number two here does exactly-as-fucking-ordered, isn't that right? Start talking. How many of you are there?" She pressed the blade still closer to the driver's neck.

"He'll kill you all," he rasped. "Alexander will make you… pay." He managed a weak cough, and I noticed his legs and lower torso were wet with blood.

"Oh, I'm gonna pay, all right," Carla sneered. "I'll pay Zander *exactly* what I owe him, don't worry. Now, answer my questions and this will be relatively painless for you"

"Fuck you," he said with another cough. "I'm not talking, and when Zander's done with you, I'm gonna enjoy"—he coughed again—"watching you die." He smiled through the pain.

"Listen, asshole," the boss said. "Whatever happens to us, you won't be around to see it, I guarantee you that. Tell us what we want to know and we'll make it quick."

The boss took a step toward the driver and reached for his throat.

The man gave a quick shudder, and his eyes snapped wide open. The half-second it took me to realize what had happened—subdermal combat stims—was a half-second too long.

He whipped Carla's hand away from his neck and rolled out the door. In a single motion, he produced a sleek black pistol from only God knows where and fired two shots, both of which hit the boss squarely in the chest. He fell hard to the ground, and I started to bring my rifle up, but the stimmed-up Section Six driver was inhumanly fast.

I didn't even have time for my life to flash before my eyes as the pistol swung in my direction, and I knew I was dead. *What a thing to die by a guy who is already dead himself when—*

The boss's revolver thundered twice from the deck, and the driver crumpled to the deck like a ragdoll.

"You all right?" I asked as I helped my boss to his feet. He nodded as he felt along his chest for bullet holes just like he had back in the truck.

"That's the last fucking time I get shot today," he managed between wheezes.

Carla slid into the driver's seat. "Well, *that's* good to know. Now what?"

"Simple," I said. "Put this thing on autopilot and send it back to home."

"And what?" the boss asked. "Just drive up guns blazing?"

I shrugged. "Why not?"

The boss stared at me, brow furrowed. "Is there a monument where you were born commemorating the birthplace of the dumbest man alive?"

"All that negativity isn't healthy, you know," I shot back.

"Neither is rolling up to a crew of heavies in a single unarmored car when we don't have any clue where they are or how many there are, Snake."

"Put his body back in the driver's seat," Carla ordered.

The boss and I answered at the same time: "Say what?"

"I've got an idea."

CHAPTER ELEVEN

I lay in the car's dark-yet-surprisingly spacious trunk, ACP clutched in my hands, finger on the trigger, and extra magazines in my pockets. Carla rode shotgun up front and practiced her crying with the dead driver in his seat. The boss lay facedown in the back floorboard, complaining that he was going to throw up from having to lie on carpet soaked in somebody else's blood. I had on the driver's bulletproof vest, which hadn't done him any good because the boss's two rounds had hit him from below and traveled up underneath his ribcage.

I hoped it would serve me better.

Carla's three-step plan was actually pretty good by my estimation.

Step one was that we'd ride in, her in tears and hysterics over the carnage she'd witnessed. Step two was for her to surrender, explaining that the boss had captured her and they'd both been in the car and then a gunfight and a knifefight and *oh God what is going on?* To sell the illusion, she'd shot a few rounds into the interior of the car, blasting out the rear passenger-side window and putting bullet holes in both rear doors. The hope was that nobody would give a second thought to the boss as he lay facedown in a pool of blood in the back of a car that looked like a slaughterhouse. Meanwhile, I'd be in the trunk, waiting to pop out like the world's worst stripper out of the world's worst birthday cake. Step three was that she would surrender to The Pale Man, convince him or otherwise con her way close enough to his computer, force him to undelete us, then kill him, somehow, I guess, while we shot it out with everybody else and then miraculously escaped.

I'll admit, it was a little short of perfect and the details were hazy, but in this business, you make do with what you've got.

I spent the twenty-minute ride pleading with various deities to let me live through this or, at the very least, kill me quickly. As I tried to remember if I'd left any gods or goddesses out, the car slowed and made a right. I felt a slight bump as the car crossed over a lip or speed bump, then a series of turns before the car stopped, followed by the sound of hydraulics and a low rumble, which I gathered was a massive door, likely a hangar door or the cargo bay door in a capital ship. My heart hammered in my chest.

Door locks clicked and the gullwing doors opened.

"What the ever-loving fuck?" a voice asked, and even through the trunk I heard the murmur of at least a dozen others.

"Don't kill me!" Carla shouted. "Please, don't kill me. I... I don't know what happened. He grabbed me and then Snake came and now..." She broke down sobbing. "And *now he's dead* and they took me to the car and there was a fight and, oh God..." Carla retched.

In the dark, I smiled. Carla was quite the actress.

My smile disappeared when I had the sudden thought that perhaps Carla's noises in bed weren't as genuine as I'd previously thought.

"Get out of the car," a harsh voice commanded. "Slowly, unless you want to look like your friend on the floorboard here."

"O-okay," Carla said, voice quivering.

"Chen, Parker, Alwei, get Peterson moved out of the car," another voice ordered. "Then put the car in there and we'll get rid of it and everything else when we hit Dubino. As for her, search her, but don't damage the goods. Alexander wants to deal with her personally. Sklyan, send word to get underway. I'll take our damsel in distress here to see the boss."

I gritted my teeth and swore under my breath, but I had no illusions about what would happen if I sprung the trap now—we'd all be cut to pieces.

A few minutes of indistinct conversation and muttered curses later, Section Six's goons had their man out of the car, and the car moved again, just a few meters across another small lip, then up an incline. Next, I heard an oddly familiar hydraulic mechanism followed by a dull thud as another door closed. I listened in silence for a few minutes but heard nothing but my pounding heart.

"Snake, you think it's safe now?" the boss whispered to me from the backseat.

"Yeah, I think so. See if you can get a look around before I pop this trunk open though."

"All right, I'll see if—holy shit, Snake. We're back!"

"What?" I asked.

"Open the trunk!"

I felt for the emergency release, pulled it, and sat up to find myself parked in a very familiar cargo bay. We were in the belly of our very own Black Sun 490. I grinned.

"Well, that solves the mystery of where they hid the ship," the boss said as he opened the gullwing door and stepped out into our cargo bay. Aside from the car taking up the space next to the cargo container we'd landed with, it didn't look like anything else had changed.

"Which is good," I said. "Because as soon as we get Carla back, I want to get the hell off this station."

"No kidding, brother," he responded. "I'm going to check on the—"

A low rumble shook everything, accompanied by the screech of metal sliding across metal. Everything lurched slightly, and a deep pulsing hum throbbed beneath our feet. The ship our Black Sun 490 was parked inside was underway. We shared a worried look.

"Shit. That complicates things," the boss said.

"Yeah, you think?"

"Actually, maybe it doesn't," the boss said, eyes narrowed in thought. "Look, we go get Carla back and get rid of our creepy bald friend—*quietly*—then we open the main cargo door and fly the ship out. Just like the old movies."

"Uh-huh, but *unlike* the old movies, if we don't cause some serious mayhem before we're gone, they're gonna hull us in like twenty seconds flat once we're out," I pointed out. "Whatever is big enough to put the Black Sun in the cargo bay has got to be like a Starskipper or a Marlin 550 at least, if not some sort of special UNF capital ship."

"So we cause some mayhem," the boss said with a shrug. "And I'd like to point out, if we open the bay door to a pressurized cargo hold when they're not expecting it? That'll be some fucking mayhem of the best kind."

"Worth a shot, I guess," I said as I followed him through the open hatch to the Black Sun's narrow crew compartment.

The boss took his familiar seat in the cockpit. He flipped a few rocker switches, and I heard the whirring of computer fans and the ship's main computer *beep* through its startup sequence from the cabinet beside me.

"Can you get this thing powered up without anybody noticing?" I asked.

He flipped a few more switches, and I heard the tapping of keys. He grunted.

"Shit. We're plugged up to their auxiliary power, which is good because I can't turn on the APU for engine or life support startup without an infernal racket. But it's also bad because as long as we're plugged up, they've got all the software on lockdown. All I've got access to is basic emergency systems. If I can get us unplugged without them noticing somehow, I could probably do an abbreviated cold start and have us outta here in say... fifteen minutes?"

"That long?" I asked. We'd taken off quicker than that a number of times under duress, and to me this seemed about as duressful as was imaginable.

"It's a cold start, Snake. Everything, and I mean, like *everything* is off. We almost never do that."

"Fuck."

"Yep."

I sighed. Somehow I knew where this conversation was going. "So let me guess, I go get Carla, kill The Pale Man, and generally fuck shit up. Meanwhile, you stay safely hidden here, get us off their network, and get everything running?"

"Pretty much."

"Something about that plan doesn't seem fair."

"She's *your* girlfriend, Snake."

"Fuck you, man."

"Well, what then? *You* want to try to stay here and do this and send me to go rescue Carla?"

I scowled. "Fine, but when I get back, this thing had better be ready to fuckin' go, because while I'll try to be quiet, I make no promises. This ain't going to be a cakewalk."

The boss nodded. "Well, it isn't going to be cakewalk for me either, because all it's going to take is one person walking into the bay for a cigarette break while I'm unscrewing the umbilical plugging us in or one system alarm and they're gonna be down here blasting at me with a fuckton of ordinance and all I've got is a coupla pistols."

I shrugged. "Well then, good luck, you bastard."

"Same to you, Snake."

I dropped down in the turret to scan for any guards, but the cavernous bay seemed deserted except for the far-off forward wall where the shadows made it too dark to see. I climbed back up.

"Let's go out the pilot's hatch," the boss suggested. "As soon as I get us unplugged, I'll get back in and lock everything up. The cockpit ought to be the most defensible position. When you come back, I'll drop the rear door."

I nodded because I was afraid that if I said anything I was going to admit that we were both probably dead men, and I didn't figure the boss needed a reminder of the obvious at the moment.

He dropped the side pilot's hatch, and we cautiously stuck our heads out into the cargo bay. "Here goes," he muttered, and I followed him down the ladder as quickly and quietly as I could.

"Hey," I said as I prepared to run across the bay, "If I'm not back in ten minutes…"

"You want me to leave?" the boss asked.

"Fuck no, you asshole," I responded in a whisper full of fury. "Of course I want you to wait until I get back! Jesus, dipshit, you think I'm gonna *ask* you to leave me and Carla aboard? Fuck that shit. If I die, you're dying with me. How long have you known me?"

I swear, this guy sometimes.

"Get the fuck out of here, Snake," the boss said with a grin. "I won't leave you. I mean, after all the shit we've been through together, I'd be distraught for probably… a couple of hours at least."

I shook my head and darted across the vast cargo bay to an open hatch reading *COMMAND QUARTERS* in stenciled letters.

I poked my head into the hatch and checked the passageway. Seeing no one, I made my way inside, rifle at the ready. I have to admit, despite my name, I didn't feel very snake-like at all. In fact, I felt like a mouse wandering around in one of those little fish tanks just waiting for something to leap out of the dark at me and bury its fangs in my neck or squeeze me around the neck till my eyes popped out of their sockets.

A set of open hatches on either side of the passage ahead gave me pause. I froze, afraid to cross the doorway, and got treated to some of the conversation from the room on the right.

"Uh-huh. Zander's gonna fuck her up good, man. I'm telling you, after what she did to him, she'll be lucky if she goes out the airlock in one piece."

"I'm glad for him, but fuck, man, this was a bloody op," a second voice answered. "Peterson, Finney, and Big C? Plus the augment team? I hope Zander's happy."

I smiled a wicked smile listening to Section Six's losses detailed. *And I'm not done yet, shitbirds.*

"He'll be happy—and you know how you'll know it?" the first voice answered. "Because you're gonna hear that bitch screaming her lungs out. Zander may have her up on A deck, bro, but you're gonna hear her down here, I swear to God."

My smile disappeared.

At least I now knew which deck I needed to get to. I gritted my teeth and darted past the door, looking for a way up.

I found a ladder just a few dozen feet ahead, set off the hallway against the hull. I looked up two decks to the A deck and down what appeared to be at least another two decks below. Not wanting to spend any more time in the passageway and growing increasingly worried about Carla, I scurried up as fast as I could, praying I didn't poke my head up onto A deck and right into the muzzle of a pistol.

My good luck continued—A deck seemed deserted. Ahead, a barely open pressure hatch beckoned, with a stenciled warning above it:

COMMANDER'S QUARTERS. AUTHORIZED PERSONNEL ONLY.

I glanced down at my mean-looking ACP. I felt pretty damn authorized.

I took a deep breath and pushed open the pressure hatch to reveal the same nicely apportioned room trimmed in wood and plush carpet where we'd first met TPM. Near the opposite wall were a few nice chairs and a massive desk. A wicked grin played across my face. I had reached The Pale Man's lair, the place that creepy sonofabitch called home. It was payback time.

I pushed the hatch almost closed behind me and, for the first time, noticed a pair of doors in the wall, colored the same flat beige as the rest of the room. I pressed my ear to the left door and heard nothing. Then I walked to the right and listened.

"So you see?" he said from inside. "There is a certain fearful symmetry about our respective positions. Karmic irony at its finest."

I heard a muffled whimper—Carla.

I kicked open the door, rifle up.

The Pale Man stood across a four-meter-by-four-meter room from me. Carla lay on a large bed, her hands and ankles bound and her mouth taped shut. The fear in her eyes changed to relief in an instant. In The Pale Man's right hand, he extended an antique silver lighter over the bed.

147

His ocular implants passed their cold gaze over me, and it was all I could do not to shiver. He looked displeased, but there was no fear. I was, to say the least, disappointed. I wanted him to shit himself, or beg, or at least look somewhat *human*.

With the flick of his thumb, a flame sprung up. My stomach lurched.

"It seems," he said in his flat tone, "that we are at an impasse. If you shoot me, this lighter will drop to the bed, igniting the mattress soaked in porophol. Are you familiar with it? Carla certainly is. She may live, but then again, she may not. Either way, she will suffer immensely. *Trust me.* It is the planned end to the festivities, but I had hoped to delay it somewhat while we caught up on our lost years."

Carla shook her head from the bed, her eyes wide with fear.

"Carla leaves with me, you creepy nightmare-fuel-looking-cybernetic shitstain," I told him. While he was no less unnerving than he had been before, the reassuring presence of an automatic weapon in my hands gave me enough confidence to talk like I had the upper hand.

"No."

"Yes. You aren't in a position to argue. I've got the rifle, and trust me when I say I will not hesitate to splatter you all across the bulkhead."

"Which would mean, you should note, that your UNF master record will be deleted," he said. "Remember, without my intervention, at the end of our ten days, you will cease to exist. Afterward, you *will* die in abject poverty and misery."

I had the sudden realization that he completely misunderstood my motivations. He didn't know me like he thought he did. I didn't know if it would save me, but the knowledge that he wasn't all-seeing and all-knowing made me feel a bit better anyway.

"I think you're confusing me with somebody who gives a fuck," I told him. "I didn't come here to save my goddamn master record. I came here to save her. And I will."

In my head, there were fireworks, patriotic music, and a flyover by the UNF Golden Hawks.

"But without—" he started.

"Save the lecture. I already told you, I don't care. The only leverage you have is lying there on that bed, and if she dies, you're dying with her— master record, ship, and whatever else be damned." I saw the briefest flash of doubt register across his corpse-like face, and I smiled.

"So let's be smart about this," I continued. "You put down the lighter, you don't delete our master records, and you do whatever Control did to hide Carla to hide us from you, and we part ways, everybody still alive. Then, you and your merry band of UNF psychos can spend the rest of your lives tracking all three of us down, and we can spend the rest of our lives in never-ending fear looking over our shoulders. That ought to be enough. People in constant terror seems to be your kink, after all."

"And what assurance do I have you will not shoot me as soon as I lower the lighter?" The Pale Man asked.

"While I'd rather die than let you keep Carla, I'd still *like* to get out of here alive, and us doing this the easy way gives me much better odds. How about that? Logic and shit, right?"

I held my breath as we stood across from one another for ten tense seconds before he closed the lighter cap, extinguishing the flame. I exhaled.

"Unlock her cuffs—and be gentle about it," I ordered. "Hurt her, and I'll blast your ass so far into the future your grandkids will be the ones to find your corpse."

The Pale Man said nothing, but hate burned in his ocular implants as he unlocked the cuffs binding her hands and feet. Carla leapt off the bed and ripped the tape off her mouth.

"You motherfucker," she snarled. "You *motherfucker*. I *loved* you Zander, once upon a time. I loved you. I *loved* you. You don't even know the meaning of the word. I was just a toy to you. You left me to worry about you with your rapey, murdering friends. Fuck you. I wish you'd stayed dead the first time I killed you."

"I will find you," The Pale Man promised, his voice loaded with such malice it made me shudder. "And when I do, I will pay you back a thousand times."

"Until then, know you were *this* close," Carla sneered, holding up her index finger and her thumb mere millimeters apart. "But I won. Again. Now, get in there to your terminal and fix their UNF master records. Hide them like Control hid me."

Carla and I kept at least an arm's distance away while he made his way out of the bedroom of horror and to his computer terminal. He sat down in the chair, called up the master records, and made a few keystrokes. The red bars around me and the boss's UNF master records marked "pending permanent removal" disappeared.

"Okay, that's one task down—now for the hiding us part," I reminded him as I kept my rifle trained on him.

"That will take more time."

"Well then, get on it. I'm not leaving until I know you won't be waiting for me the next place I land."

He didn't answer, fingers flashing over the keyboard and calling up a dizzying array of menus and command screens.

Three stern knocks sounded on the hatch door. I froze. My eyes met Carla's, and I'm sure the horrified expression on her face mirrored my own.

Shit.

The Pale Man looked at me, and the corners of his mouth turned up in the faintest of smiles. I shook my head.

"Not now," The Pale Man told whoever was at his door.

"It's important, Alexander," the intruder said as the door swung open.

Instinctively, I swung the rifle to cover the door. A startled member of Section Six froze in the doorway, and I caught a flash of white from the corner of my eye. I tried to bring the rifle back around to The Pale Man, but I was too late.

He grabbed Carla with one arm and swatted my rifle away with the other. She tried to duck out of his grasp and landed a solid blow to his midsection. While they wrestled for advantage, the Section Six agent in the doorway unholstered his pistol. I dove for the ground as shots punched into the wall beside me.

I fired poorly aimed bursts at the doorway that sent bullets ricocheting down the corridor, and the gunfire nearly deafened me. The Pale Man and Carla's struggle took them off their feet and crashing through the doorway back into the bedroom.

The Section Six goon reappeared in the doorway, firing off another two shots and sending me scrambling behind the desk for cover. I fired another burst.

From inside the bedroom, Carla screamed.

No, no, no, no, no.

I threw myself through the doorway into the bedroom, another round cracking past me and burying itself in the wall.

The Pale Man had Carla in a chokehold against him with one hand while he struggled to subdue her flailing arms with the other. Before I could get my rifle up, he kicked me in the face with his left boot hard enough to make me see stars. His next kick sent my ACP tumbling to the floor.

He must have anticipated I'd go for the rifle because he delivered a blow that likely would have knocked me out had I reached for it. Instead, I jerked back, grabbed his leg, and pushed upward, which sent him careening off balance.

Carla twisted out of his grip, smashed her elbow into his face, and pushed him back into the bed. His head came up first as he tried to get away, his scarred face a twisted mask of rage, but Carla punched him hard in the temple. As I scooped my rifle off the floor, silver flashed in Carla's hand, and I caught a glimpse of a tongue of yellow flame.

The Pale Man's rage turned to horror as Carla dropped the lighter into the bed.

The subsequent *whoosh* sent Carla and me staggering backward from the pyre. The Pale Man gave an inhuman shriek of pain and defeat. He stretched a burning arm toward us, whether looking for help or to drag us into the flame with him I couldn't say. Carla snatched the ACP from me and fired a burst into his flaming body as he writhed on the bed. The Pale Man's shrieking ended abruptly.

"Paid in full, you son of a bitch," she whispered. "Paid in fucking full."

She handed the rifle back to me, and I poked my head out the bedroom door, almost catching a slug in the teeth from the Section Six agent who'd kept his position in the outer doorway.

I fired a long burst from the ACP, this one zipping clean through the steel bulkhead and into the agent in the doorway. He dropped face first into the room and lay still.

Leaving the dead behind, Carla and I bolted for the hatch, pausing only long enough for her to grab the agent's pistol. We ran pell-mell for the ladder. A head popped through the hatch, and Carla fired at it. She missed, but the man shouted in fright, and I heard a few loud bangs and a nasty crunch as the agent lost his footing and fell down several decks below. I grabbed Carla and pointed down the ladder.

"We got to go down! The hangar bay is on C deck."

I climbed down the ladder first, pulse pounding and adrenaline pumping, hoping not to run into anybody armed coming up. Carla clambered after me until we reached C deck, where we ran back toward the hangar bay.

Three people in the passageway loomed suddenly out of a doorway in front of us, looking just as shocked to see us as we were to see them. Carla and I both fired, dropping two of them and sending the third diving back into the room. Between the gunfire and the echoes I felt like my ears were bleeding.

Once we made it to the cargo bay, our Black Sun seemed farther away than I remembered. We took off toward it at a dead sprint, ignoring shouts from the passageway behind us and an incoherent yell from a catwalk above.

A bullet snapped past me and another *spranged* off the deck beside. Carla extended her pistol behind her and fired without aiming, but I just kept my legs pumping. Ahead, the rear cargo door opened.

A hammer blow hit me in the back, knocking the wind out of me and sending me sprawling to the deck. If it hurt that bad being shot *with* a vest, I had no desire to find out what it was like being shot without one. I scrambled forward on all fours until I reached the Black Sun's rear door. There, I crouched next to the rear right strut and used it for cover while I sprayed a long burst at a pair of figures running after us. They crumpled to the ground.

"Yo, boss, we're back!" I shouted. "Let's get the fuck outta here!"

"There's been an unfortunate change of plans," the boss said, his voice strangely muffled.

I fired another burst at the doorway and a shorter one at the catwalk above and slightly forward before I risked a look at the boss. He wore his full EVP suit, and Carla was helping him throw in spare oxygen bottles along with what looked to be the entire contents of our clothes locker into a meter-and-a-half-by-meter-and-a-half shipping crate.

"What the hell is going on?" I demanded.

"I don't have time to explain, Snake. Get into yours." He pointed to the ship's second environmental protection suit laid out on the cargo bay floor.

A round pinged off the ship, but I didn't move.

"What are you doing?" I asked.

He ignored me. "Carla, take over the gun from Snake and keep them off us while I get this going."

"Again, *what* is going on?" I asked as Carla took the rifle from my hands and a spare mag from my pocket.

The boss shook his head, frustration visible through the suit's helmet. He disappeared back inside and went forward toward the cockpit. I followed. "Bossman, talk to me, what are—"

"Your suit, Snake. Put it on, goddamn it!" he thundered before he went through the hatch into the crew compartment.

Carla fired a burst, and I heard a cry of pain from across the hangar bay.

"That's right, fuckers!" she shouted. "Stay back unless you want some more." She fired another burst, and more rounds bounced off our ship in response.

Bewildered, I struggled into the bright yellow EVP suit designed for emergency evacuation situations or external maintenance in deep space. Carla seemed to have things under control, so I went looking for the boss. He was in the cockpit, running through some sequence I wasn't familiar with, bathed in the light of red warning lights. It took a second, but then I realized what he was doing.

"You're gonna eject the jump drive?" I asked.

He grunted.

"But… why? I mean, it will breach their ship, sure, but it'll contain and they'll be emergency repressurized as soon as we open the cargo door. Why aren't we flying out like—"

"Because we can't," he snapped. "Even after I unplugged the umbilical, the systems won't restart. Some kind of security setting I can't break. The motherfuckers got me, okay, Snake? I still can't access anything but emergency systems. I can't even turn on the APU or engines or comms or even get past the startup subroutine or any of that shit, all right? But I can eject the core."

Carla fired another burst, and I risked poking my head out into the cargo bay, looking out the open cargo ramp and plotting a course for the ejected jump core. At the angle we sat in their cargo hold, the jump drive would punch a hole in the rear quarter of the massive freighter, doing no small amount of monetary damage and probably taking a few lives with it, but nowhere near enough to keep the ship from flying or to prevent us from being turned inside out by their laser turrets as we drifted outside in our EVP suits.

"I don't get it, boss," I said. "We're still gonna die. And Carla doesn't even have a suit."

"Nope, she doesn't," he said as he ran through a series of menus and flipped a couple of rocker switches. "She's going to have to make do in the crate. It's airtight. She's got the spare ox tanks, some blankets, and the emergency chemical heaters. It's all we've got."

"Hey, boys?" Carla yelled. "They've retreated for the time being, but something tells me they're just licking their wounds and we're not gonna like what comes next. Whatever your plan is, ace, you'd better get on it."

"I gotcha," the boss called back. "Get in the shipping container and get ready for a ride. All we gotta do is open the cargo door and—"

"You're not serious," Carla said. "*That's* the plan? We're gonna drift out so they can pick us off?"

"I'm going to eject the jump drive core."

"But without main power you won't have— *ooooh.*" Her eyebrows rose. "Shit, you got balls, if not brains," Carla said.

I was still lost. I knew you could eject the jump core at incredibly high speed as a safety precaution in case it overheated and started going critical, but I didn't understand how that was going to help us here.

"Somebody explain what the hell's going on," I said. "Goddamn it, I'm about to die and I deserve to know how."

"The jump drive is ninety-nine percent of the mass of any ship, right, Snake?" Carla asked from the hold.

"Well, actually, it's ninety-eight point five," the boss pointed out.

"Whatever," she said. "Anyway, the thing is massive and ejects out of the ship at something like—"

"Yeah, yeah, twenty-five kilometers per second, I know," I interrupted. "I know it's gonna tear a sweet-ass hole through the back part of their ship and space some people, but that ain't gonna do this baby in, not by a long shot."

"Uh-huh," Carla agreed. "But without main power from the engines providing damping for the jump core, there's no force acting against it. Think about the laws of motion."

"I skipped that class."

"When the jump core evacs at twenty-five kps that way"—Carla stood up so I could see her through the hatch and pointed out the rear of the ship—"the rest of the ship has gotta go *that* way." She pointed forward. I had a sudden flash of understanding.

"At close to twenty-five kps," I finished.

"Yeah," the boss said from his seat. "Whatever restraints they have the Black Sun in ain't gonna hold up to that much force. Which means no more ship for us. Because this thing is going to disintegrate as it punches a hole right through the entire forward half of their ship and probably trigger a catastrophic reactor failure. Plus, the, uh, giant-ass hull breach."

"So we're gonna die," I said as matter-of-factly as I could.

"Most likely, yeah. But not *definitely*. Because we're going to be hanging on to Carla's shipping container on the zero-g cargo transfer lift, which means, *theoretically*, when the ship goes forward and it yanks their whole ship forward with it, we sit still. So, the ship blasts forward, drags them along, and as that happens we stay right here and go right through the cargo bay door and into space. You get it?"

"But the—"

"Oh, yeah," the boss added, "and hopefully nothing blows up until it's far enough away so we don't get turned into a plasma cloud."

"Well, shit."

"Yep. Now come on."

I followed him back to the cargo hold, and Carla climbed into the shipping container, handing the rifle to me. The boss and I sealed it and made sure it was properly positioned on the maglev cargo handler so that when he disengaged the mag lock prior to ejecting the jump core, we'd all be levitating a few frictionless centimeters above the ship's surface.

"Now what?" I asked.

"Well, there's a small—"

It hit me. "Wait. Their cargo bay door is still closed. Which means we get smashed into it unless…"

"*Now* you've got it. So one of us runs out to the far end of the cargo bay and opens the manual controls, which I've already disabled the safeties on, and one of us stays here and guards the ship."

"All right, I'm gone," I said. I handed him the ACP.

"I was gonna do it, Snake," the boss called after me.

"You're too slow!" I shouted back.

———————————

You ever run in a full EVP suit on in a pressurized hull in full grav? It's a hazing ritual on most ships, if that tells you anything. The cargo bay seemed to stretch on forever in front of me as I ran so hard I thought my damn heart was going to explode. Halfway to the panel, with no cover anywhere close, I heard a pair of *snaps* as two bullets cracked past me.

Dear God, I prayed, not now. Not here. Not after I've saved Carla from the devil incarnate. Not now. It would be cruel to kill me before I get laid after this adventure, because it's going to be epic.

Another long burst of gunfire *zinged* off the deck in front of me. God, it seemed, was not in a listening mood.

I heard the staccato burst of the ACP and then the hiss of something slicing through the air. I looked back just in time to see a shoulder-fired rocket slam into the side of the Black Sun 490. Fortunately, its warhead appeared to have been too small to do any real damage, but it was a disconcerting escalation in terms of hardware they seemed willing to use indoors.

"Motherfuckers," I wheezed as I ran. "Don't blow up our ship. Only we're allowed to do that."

Another round zipped past me, then another, and another. I had the feeling someone understood what I was trying to do. On instinct, I threw myself prone.

And just in time. A rocket screamed above me, impacting the far bay door with a spray of spalling shrapnel.

I got to my feet and sprinted the remaining distance, almost throwing up from the exertion. At the control panel, I threw open the switch cover marked with yellow and black caution markings and ignored at least a dozen warnings not to flip the switch. I grabbed the nearby safety hold and flipped it.

Nothing happened.

Goddamn it, what now?

I flinched as another bullet tore past me. It was only then that noticed a red box glowing on a nearby touch screen: *ARE YOU SURE YOU WISH TO OPEN CARGO BAY DOOR? WARNING: PRESSURE DIFFERENCE DETECTED AND ALL BAY ACCESS HATCHES ARE NOT SEALED.*

I made sure I had a good grip on the safety hold again and touched the red box labeled *CONFIRM.*

The huge bay doors in front of me parted as the pressure difference blasted the air out at gale force, sending debris, empty containers, and several limp bodies sliding past me and into the darkness of the void. Klaxons sounded but grew distant and faint as the air rushed past me. A series of warning lights lit the now silent cargo bay.

With the flow of air rushing past me slowing, I began my run back to our waiting Black Sun 490. Ahead, a pair of figures clung to an overhead catwalk, apparently to prevent themselves from being sucked out. I didn't feel any sympathy for the bastards when they dropped to the deck floor below for lack of oxygen. In the vacuum, they didn't even make any noise when they hit.

As I jogged back, I noticed all the hatches had automatically closed, sealing us inside the bay—at least as long as it took the crew to get into their EVP suits and come back out, guns blazing. Although I knew we had no intention of waiting that long, I was starting to wonder if I'd rather face gunfire than what we had planned.

Back on the Black Sun, the boss helped me cinch to the shipping pallet. When we were both securely tied, he picked up a long rope that disappeared through the hatch and into the crew compartment, attached to what I figured was the jump core emergency evacuation handle in the cockpit.

He grimaced through his EVP helmet, then shook his head. The boss tripped the maglock switch to his right, and I felt the sensation of weightlessness as the cargo container we were attached to rose slightly.

The boss had tears in his eyes, and even though I couldn't hear him in the vacuum conditions, I was able to make out a single silent word, not to me but to the ship: *Bye*.

He tugged the cord.

The only experience I'd ever had to compare what it felt like was when I was in a train crash on Yiemos right after I finished my time aboard the

Braxton. Even though in theory the magnetic zero-g cargo was frictionless, it didn't *quite* work out that way in practice. A sudden jerk—like god had ripped my skeleton from my body—made me see double and sloshed what little brains I hadn't already managed to drink away. I felt like my head was going to come off my neck. The ships, both ours and theirs, vanished in a blur of gray and white and blue, and I barely kept from throwing up in my EVP suit from the sudden, dizzying sensation of speed disorientation. The three of us tumbled end over end in the void, and as the world spun around, I was treated to two sights over and over and over again.

One was Bohr Station itself, distant but still easily seen, its windows and hangar bays pinpricks of light against the darkness of space. The other was a rapidly expanding yellow ball of flame, with hints of violet and deep red plasma dancing across its face.

CHAPTER TWELVE

The detective who sat across the table from me was not amused.

"Again, do you recognize this person?" The detective held up a picture of the boss.

"Nope."

"Uh-huh. You do realize that was the man you were found alongside wearing an EVP in the middle of the nav lane, right?"

I shrugged.

He sighed and then held up a picture of Carla. "Do you recognize her?"

"Nope."

"She was the woman who was in the shipping container you two were found tied to."

"Huh, fancy that," I said. "She's pretty hot. You got her number?"

"What about this?" The detective held up a picture of a highly customized late model Indus Starfreighter that I presumed had recently been the property of the late Section Six and that had served The Pale Man's mobile command post.

"Got me, man."

"You can't tell me *anything* about this picture?" he said, bewildered frustration seeping into his voice.

"Nah."

"Anything at all?"

"I'm gonna go out on a limb and say that's a spacecraft." I smiled my biggest shit-eating grin and took another sip of coffee. Playing the most ignorant man alive was fun with the cops, and not very hard for me, seeing as how I spent most of my time flying around with the *actual* most ignorant man alive. That may seem harsh to the boss, but I was pretty sure he was two rooms over thinking and doing the same thing.

"Does the name Alexander Corbin mean anything to you?" he asked, more resigned this time than frustrated.

"Nope."

"You know that lying to deputized law officers of Bohr Security carries a sentence of six months, and that doing it in relation to a UNF matter bumps it up to a federal charge, where you're looking at a minimum of three years, right?"

I pretended to mull that over before I responded. "Didn't know that either."

"Look, you little shit, if I so much as find you've got an overdue docking fee within six jumps I'm going to lock you up for a year," the detective snarled. "Is there anything you *do* know?"

I finished my coffee, which felt good. I'd yet to unthaw from our two hours tumbling and drifting, a duration that, while it was within the rated timeline of the EVP suits, was pushing it just a bit. I didn't answer.

The detective slammed his fist on the table. "Goddamn it, *answer me*. I asked you if there was anything you do know?"

"Fine. Yeah, here's what I know. I know that I'm not saying shit, and I know that you're gonna walk out there and ask to keep me anyway." I nodded to the rest of the station outside the interrogation room. "Then, I know your boss is gonna tell you that you can't because you've got no reason to hold me 'cause floating through space tied to a shipping container isn't a crime. Then I know you're gonna let me go. *That's* what I know, so be about it so I can get out of here." I gave him the most serene, infuriating smile I could muster.

He snorted and pushed himself away from the table.

Just as he yanked the door open, I stopped him with a raised hand. "Hey, I will tell you one thing."

He let the door close and turned back to me. "What's that?"

"You guys are better baristas than you are cops, because this coffee is *damn* good. Consider that some career advice." I winked and raised my coffee cup, and he slapped it out of my hand. I chuckled. It was empty anyway.

Five minutes later, I found myself standing outside the police office on the Bohr Station Administration District on B Deck, in a concourse full of shops and restaurants that served the station's various government agencies. I lit a cigarette and scanned through the crowds, trying to find the cheapest looking bar. I settled on one, made my way through the sea of people to its entrance, and was rewarded by seeing Carla and the boss at a table through the window. I ducked inside.

As I slid into the booth next to Carla, I noticed the boss already had several whiskey tumblers in front of him. Carla had none.

"What took you two so long?" the boss asked as he polished off another glass of what I guessed was scotch. The way he almost knocked another glass off the table when he slammed the tumbler down told me he was already feeling it.

"I didn't think it was that long," I said. "I stonewalled 'em and they let me go."

"Yeah, me too," agreed Carla. "I told 'em I didn't know shit, didn't remember shit, and wasn't interested in finding shit out either."

"The real question," I asked my half-drunk boss, "is how did you get released so quick?"

"Simple. I told 'em everything."

"You *what*?" Carla said.

The boss shrugged. "Yeah, I tried to tell 'em the truth. Figured maybe if I could get 'em to believe me, I could file suit against the UNF and get enough money to buy a new ship."

"You went to the stupid fountain and took a long drink, didn't you?" Carla asked with a shake of her purple hair. "That's not how things work, ace, and I figured anybody in your line of work would know that. The cops and the courts aren't going to believe you because they never do, and the UNF sure as hell isn't going to acknowledge Section Six, since everybody knows they don't exist, and if they *did* say Section Six existed, the UNF would be settling lawsuits from now until doomsday. You'd have better luck shaking down Snake's broke ass for cash."

"Hey," I interjected with a playful elbow into Carla's ribs.

"What? It's true, isn't it?"

I considered that. "Fair point."

"Well, I still had hopes," the boss said with a scowl. "Didn't work, obviously. As soon as I said 'Section Six' they kicked me out of the station with a pair of business cards for local mental health counselors and a court-ordered appointment with a psychiatrist."

"You know," I said with a smile, "you should probably take them up on the psychiatrist appointment."

"Ha-motherfucking-ha. Aren't you the funnyman, Snake." He signaled the waitress, who brought him another whiskey double.

I knew what was going on. Even though I felt the loss of the ship pretty keenly, I had the prospect of some mind-blowing alone time with Carla coming up and the boss had... nothing, really. The ship was both our lives, in a manner of speaking, but it was *everything* to the boss. Without it, he was just another pilot taking jobs for whoever would have him, cutting points off his rate and break time between runs to try to beat the other guy or, even worse, working for one of the sector's big shipping companies making the same run day in and day out.

In our line of work, there's captain-owners and then there's everybody else.

"Look, man, we'll work something out," I tried to reassure him as he downed half the glass. "We'll get hired on and do some local runs for a bit and save up enough—"

The boss snorted. He knew my plan was bullshit probably even more than I did. He finished his whiskey and leaned back with a sigh. "You can't save up enough for a ship doing local runs, Snake, and you know it. If it was that easy, every dick out there would be flying for himself, but notice that shit doesn't happen, does it?"

"No, I guess not."

I motioned to the waitress, pointed at the boss's empty glasses, and held up three fingers. She nodded and disappeared. Nobody said anything until she came back with more whiskeys. I drank mine in a single pull—I was more of a bourbon guy than a scotch guy, but I'm hardly what you'd call picky. As the whiskey warmed me, I tried to think of a way out of the very sobering reality the boss was making it impossible to ignore.

"I've got a solution," Carla said softly. "But, um…"

I gave her a surprised look. "You do?"

"Yeah, let's hear it, Carla," the boss said.

"Well, it's like this. I've got a pretty good amount saved up, and, well, living the kind of life I do, I've missed out on some things, you know?" Her eyes cut to me. I felt myself in a very unfamiliar situation. Was Carla saying she'd been missing *me*? I was flattered, if more than a bit unnerved. Most of my relationships have been fleeting and more than a few have been what one might call "transactional."

"Uh-huh, and?" the boss said, seemingly oblivious to what I was pretty sure Carla meant.

"The Rais are looking to start up a training school for their own armed escorts. Not an armed wing, exactly, but they'd rather have their own people flying for them on their pilgrimages than a bunch of hired guns, on account of some trouble they've had in that arena. Hell, this last bit I was flying for them we lost two mid-job to better contracts, and one of the others turned out to be selling their movement data to quadrant sec. I've done good work for them, and the pilgrimage leader told me anytime me or anybody I recommended wanted the job, it was theirs."

"You're suggesting I go sign up as a trainer to teach a bunch of loonies how to fly?" the boss asked incredulously.

"No," Carla said. "I'm not saying you should. I'm saying *I* should." There was a half a beat before she said what she really meant. "And Snake."

I felt that was my cue to talk, but my brain was doing too much calculation to process any words. What was Carla saying? What did she *mean*? What was I supposed to say? Was I supposed to say anything?

"So how does you running off with my partner help me get—" the boss began.

"You can have the Razor," Carla said.

My mouth dropped open. Her Razor combat shuttle was top of the line. That ship was the fighter jet to our Black Sun 490's buggy pulled by a lazy, asthmatic horse. Used, it was worth four times what our ancient Black Sun had been worth brand new.

The boss blinked like she'd just offered to fuck him, which I think would have been even less surprising to him than her offering to give up her ship.

"The—*your*—Razor?" the boss stammered. "You're going to give me a ship in exchange for... *Snake*?"

"Pretty much, yeah."

The boss looked at me, a befuddled look on his face. "Uh, Snake?"

I give him credit for not just saying "yes" right off the bat. Hell, *I'd* trade me for a Razor and consider myself to have swindled who'd ever given up the Razor, and I think I'm a pretty cool guy.

The intensity of the looks I got from Carla and the boss could have melted steel. I finished the dregs of whiskey in my glass before I answered.

Underneath the table, I grabbed Carla's hand. "I'm in."

Carla and I, alone in dark clothes and pants among the swirl of colored saris and song, stood out on the gangplank of the Rai *Laughter's Harvest*, as did the boss as he fought his way through the crowd toward us.

When he reached us, he shook his head with a grin. "You're really gonna do this, Snake? You gonna be wearing a yellow-flower-print sari and going on about the 'Oneness of the Rai' next time I run into you?"

"Hell no," I said. "I'm working for these dudes, not joining them. How long have you known me?"

"Look," the boss told Carla, "he's a pain in the ass to live with, and you'll probably regret this deal two days from now, but no takebacks, got it?"

She chuckled and rolled her eyes. "Don't sweat it. I can handle him."

I smiled. "And trust me, I can handle her. Shit. Last night, you shoulda—"

Carla jabbed me in the ribs, hard. "Keep talking and that'll be your 'last night' for a long while, asshole."

"I'm shutting up."

"Jesus. I'm glad somebody can make you," the boss said. He turned serious. "Snake, you and Carla ever run into trouble, just let me know and I'll do what I can."

"Which, given our history together, probably means make it worse," I noted.

"True."

We stood, facing each other without saying anything for a moment. I heard an electronic *beep*, and the boss glanced down at the watch implanted in his wrist.

"Shit," he said. "I gotta go. Got our final preflight meeting with the guys I'm escorting in like half an hour."

"No problem," I told him. "We're about to shove off here too. Just remember when you're out there, you won't have me to bail you out with my superior gunnery skills."

"Where have you been keeping those?" he asked. "Because I've sure as hell never seen 'em. I'll survive."

He stuck out his hand.

I took it, pulled him close, and we clapped each other's backs. When we parted, I noticed Carla looked a little misty-eyed. I shook my head.

"Been a hell of a run, Snake," the boss said.

"Yeah, man, it has."

"The galaxy's a small place. See you around sometime."

"You know it. Seriously, take care of yourself."

"You too," he said.

"Yep."

About the Author

David Dixon has been writing fiction and non-fiction for over twenty years. A husband, father of two, and Army veteran whose combat days are long behind him, he lives in Northern Virginia where he writes across a variety of genres and topics. He believes that for every person and every place, there's a story, whether it's a comedy, tragedy, or something in between—and it's his hope to write them all.

More From
Dark Brew Press and
David Dixon

The Damsel
(Black Sun #1)

After a hijacking attempt damages their decrepit Black Sun 490 freighter, Snake and his boss are desperate for cash.

Enter Carla, a gorgeous mercenary bad girl with a job offer that seems too good to be true. Unfortunately for him, while Snake is convinced she's stringing them along to their deaths, he's not the one in charge.

The job gets dicey in a hurry, and it doesn't take him long to figure out a fatal blow is coming. He's just not sure if it will come from the pirates that haunt the nav lanes, knife-wielding goons looking for revenge, Carla herself, or the cheap vodka he drinks to stay sane.

If Snake's going to make it out alive, he'll need every bit of his quick wit—and an even quicker trigger finger.

Six-Gun Shuffle
(Black Sun #2)

Snake and the boss have made a lot of enemies, but up until their trip to Yaeger, they've never had any beef with Michael Ver, the galaxy's most bankable popstar—mainly because they hadn't met him before. After the boss teaches Ver a lesson about the difference between looking tough and being tough, he finds himself a minor viral video star and catches the eye of a gorgeous redhead named Kell.

Things are looking up.

That is, until Kell goes missing and the boss goes after her. After a shootout with Ver's crew, things go from bad to worse—nobody can find Ver, and Snake and the boss are the prime suspects in his disappearance.

The next thing they know they've got a bounty on their heads and hardly a friend in sight. Carla and Kell are the only people they can count on, but has Kell been playing a different game all along? It's a mixed-up tale of bounty hunters, crooked cops, popstars and… insurance agents?

More From Dark Brew Press

Urban Gothic
by Stephen Coghlan

Burned out and drugged up, Alec LeGuerrier spends his days faking it, barely ekeing out an existence while living in a haze of confusion and medicated mellowness. That is, until he stops a gang of nightmarish oddities from killing a strange young woman with indigo eyes.

Dragged into the lands of the dreaming, he must come to terms with his brutal past and his grim imagined future in a land his body knows is real, but his mind refuses to acknowledge.

The Cranes of Blackwell by J.D. Kellner

Bergden and Alyssa Crane are dutiful citizens of the Regime. Bergden, a Regime blackjack and Alyssa, a faithful wife, do what they can to provide for their son, James even when it means sacrificing their very freedom. But when Bergden is accused of treason, the Cranes must flee for their lives to escape the terrible reach of the Regime. During the escape, Bergden and Alyssa become separated.

Now, Bergden and Alyssa will do whatever they must, and against all odds, to unite their family. With the tyrannical Chancellor Kroft hunting them night and day, both must discover their inner strengths to conquer their fears and find each other's arms.

Little do they realize that a greater threat lurks in the shadows.

Lightning Source UK Ltd.
Milton Keynes UK
UKHW010631140622
404409UK00001B/177